Drawn to Life

Drawn to Life

Elisabeth Wagner

Translated by Julia Knobloch

amazon crossing

This is a work of fiction. Names, characters, organizations, places, events, and incidents are either products of the author's imagination or are used fictitiously.

Text copyright © 2013 Elisabeth Wagner

Translation copyright © 2015 Julia Knobloch

All rights reserved.

No part of this book may be reproduced, or stored in a retrieval system, or transmitted in any form or by any means, electronic, mechanical, photocopying, recording, or otherwise, without express written permission of the publisher.

Previously published as *Bring mich Heim* by Amazon Publishing in Germany in 2013. Translated from German by Julia Knobloch. First published in English by AmazonCrossing in 2015.

Published by AmazonCrossing, Seattle

www.apub.com

Amazon, the Amazon logo, and AmazonCrossing are trademarks of Amazon.com, Inc., or its affiliates.

ISBN-13: 9781477827574
ISBN-10: 1477827579

Cover design by Laura Klynstra

Library of Congress Control Number: 2014919939

Printed in the United States of America

Every day deserves to be fought for.
Breathe!
Live!

I had everything I could think of. I was doing great.

I was self-confident. I had the best friends ever. A fantastic job. A stable relationship. My first apartment.

I had a future.

And then . . . what was left?

I . . . I was all that was left.

But I hated myself.

Mia

Prologue
Mia—Graduation Day

Graz, June 2010

I had made it. Years of studying were finally over. No more sitting at my desk, hour after hour, buried in books. The library I'd acquired during my time in college disappeared in moving boxes, stored away in my parents' attic, abandoned to dust and oblivion.

Now in my early twenties, I'd finished my studies and earned my degree. After laboring for three years, finally my last day of college had arrived. I'd enjoyed being a student. Among many good memories were some not-so-great ones, but I wouldn't change a thing. Each experience had made me the person I was. The person I wanted to be. I was happy and proud . . . For twenty-three, I'd achieved a lot. Nobody could take this away from me.

Everything seemed perfect. During school, I'd landed an internship with the press office of the local newspaper, which had proven the ideal job for me. I was a very outgoing person and loved to come up with new ideas about how to promote the newspaper and how to connect people.

Then things got even better. My internship turned into a full-time position. I was ecstatic. I'd found my calling.

I was so happy that I couldn't stop smiling on commencement day.

"Can you believe it, Mia?" My friend Julia jumped up and down. Apparently I wasn't the only one feeling high that day. "It's over. No more studying ever again. I was beginning to think we would never graduate."

I smiled. She and I didn't need many words; we understood each other without saying a thing. Besides, my expression displayed my joyfulness much better than words.

Our newfound freedom felt surreal. Never again would we set foot in this building. We'd made it! All those all-nighters had been well worth the struggle.

"Come on! Let's get out of these gowns and meet the guys. I'm sure they're already waiting."

"You don't need to tell me twice," I said, grinning at my best friend.

We helped each other out of the huge, itchy, tentlike gowns, though the getup, especially with the cap, had made me feel very important. Then Julia took my hand and dragged me through the crowd and out the door.

"Hey there, beautiful! Are you ready for a surprise?"

Christoph, my boyfriend of three years, hugged me from behind and placed a tender kiss on the nape of my neck.

"You're a knockout in that business suit. You should wear it more often," he whispered in my ear. I craned my neck to look at him. "Babe, I'm very proud of you. You've earned a reward."

I turned around slowly, still in his embrace. Smiling, I wrapped my arms around his neck and softly kissed his mouth. Even after several years with him, I still couldn't get enough of those lips. Tenderly, rising on my toes, my own skimmed up his cheek until they reached his left ear.

"Now, *that* surprise, I can clearly picture," I whispered and nibbled playfully at his earlobe.

"Mimi, baby, you are driving me crazy," he muttered hoarsely. His hands wandered down the small of my back and touched my butt.

I leaned in closer, but he loosened his grip, took my hand, and said, "OK guys, let's hit the road before it gets too late. Markus, Julia, let's go!"

Tuscany, June 2010

"Stop teasing and tell us where we're going," I begged Christoph and Markus, Julia's boyfriend.

"Nope." Sitting shotgun, Markus let his head fall back against the seat as he laughed. Strands of his black hair swept over his forehead. He turned around to look at Julia and me. I glanced at Christoph. An equally broad smile was plastered on my boyfriend's face.

Julia pouted. "You're so cruel. We're going on a trip, right? Why else would we need baggage?" she asked.

The two guys apparently couldn't help themselves. Their laughter grew louder. Julia and I sat with our arms crossed and glared. Then I poked Christoph's shoulder, raised my eyebrows, and made a pretense of scolding him. "Do you have any idea what a pain it is for women to pack their bags without a clue where they're going? Just so you know, everything I own is in there, and I don't want to hear a single complaint that it's too heavy. Do you understand? Why, we could be going somewhere freezing cold!"

My boyfriend shook his head. "Are you serious? You're telling me that you packed winter clothes?"

"That's exactly what I'm telling you."

Julia pursed her lips, but I could tell she was trying not to laugh.

"Hofi," Christoph addressed Markus by his nickname, "my girlfriend is insane. Winter clothes?" With wide eyes he looked at me in the rearview mirror. "You've got to be kidding."

Julia couldn't resist any longer and her merriment spilled out.

"Well, that's what you get when you don't tell us our destination. Next time just add *warm* or *cold*. It'll make things so much easier."

Now Markus grinned along with Christoph. "Juli, please tell me you didn't bring winter clothes, too." Running his fingers through his wavy hair, he shook his head and sighed.

Christoph threw me a crooked smile. "Letting you gals know would have spoiled the whole surprise, so I'll take full responsibility for your heavy bag." He winked at me.

Seven hours later, we knew we would definitely not need our sweaters. Our boyfriends were treating us to a vacation in Italy! After the long hours in the car, my legs felt numb and my back hurt. I yawned and stretched my stiff bones. But who cared? We were in Tuscany!

I threw my arms around Christoph's neck and covered his face with kisses. "Thank you, thank you, thank you . . . ! This is so sweet of you. My darling, you're the absolute best. I love you so much."

Christoph removed a strand of hair from my face and stroked my cheek with his thumb. His soft lips caressed mine. My heart beat faster. Brushing back a lock of his soft blond hair, I took a deep breath, inhaling his familiar smell, and held him tighter. He leaned his forehead against mine and looked into my eyes.

"I would do anything for you." His smile broadened. "I love you, too, Mimi."

I still got goose bumps every time he said those three magic words.

We spent a whole week in Italy. Though Markus and Christoph had organized the trip together, while we were there, each couple went off alone with their partners, then reunited as a foursome for dinner.

I knew Tuscany only from photos and friends' travel descriptions. Now I was finally there myself, ready to have my own experiences and to take my own pictures. I planned to draw a lot, too—something I loved to do. I couldn't wait to explore the medieval cities, to feel that special feeling, that one you get when your fingertips touch a wall that is many, many centuries old.

The trip started out in Pisa where, to be honest, what I wanted most was to have that one photograph taken that everyone has taken while visiting that city. You know the one—where someone pretends to push against the Leaning Tower, as if to stop it from tipping over. True enough, it was the first thing we did. Without that snapshot, I would have refused to move on.

Once this important task had been checked off, we visited the Piazza del Duomo and then the romantic cathedral of Santa Maria Assunta, with its interior lined with splendid frescos. Christoph's hand in mine, I stared at the ceiling for what seemed forever, in silent awe. Words could not express how I felt.

Our next stop was Livorno. We spent the entire first day at the beach, on an empty stretch Christoph and Markus found, an ideal place to unwind and relax. It was heaven. With the sun warming my body and the breezes from the Mediterranean assuring I wasn't too hot, I sat back in my new bikini on my colorful towel and dug my toes into the sand.

Christoph hugged me from behind, kissing my neck and my shoulder, and whispering sweet words in my ear. "I love you so, so much. I can never get enough of you."

I laughed and twisted to look at him. "Enough of me or enough of this?" I motioned to my body.

He shook his head in mock disapproval. "Whoever said men have only one thing on their minds was wrong."

I shrugged, leaned in closer to kiss him, and—bumped against the hard sand instead. He'd jumped to his feet and was trotting off. Startled, I watched him.

He looked back at me over his shoulder. "You'll have to work for this kiss!" he shouted, laughter in the words.

Quickly I rose to chase after him, but he turned the tables and ran after me. Realizing he intended to throw me in the sea, I screamed and tried to escape. But I wasn't nearly as fast as he was. He easily caught up and, before I knew it, had slung me over his shoulder. He ran fast and wild as my hair fell over my face, and I squealed the surf grew closer and closer. Then he halted, only to whirl us around.

I laughed.

"Chris, stop it! You're making me dizzy!"

He only laughed harder and whirled us around faster. "Sounds good to me!"

With a huge splash, we hit the waves. As I sank underwater, I opened my eyes. Christoph's eyes were open, too. Our gazes met. He swam closer and grabbed my hips, and we rose together above the surface.

For a long time, we just looked at each other, grinning with happiness. I loved his smile, now reflected in his wide brown eyes. I could never get enough of him. He was my Christoph. Kind, attentive, and always there for me. I so adored him.

The remaining day we had left in Livorno was clearly not enough time to do the city's sights justice, but we'd never regret spending so long at the beach. Although we had less time than initially planned, we did manage to explore the historic district, especially Venezia Nuova—New Venice—known for its narrow, navigable canals.

The next stop was Volterra. I knew Christoph had included this stop only for my sake. He liked to tease me about my infatuation with the place. The book *New Moon* was set there, and every time I read the novel or watched the movie, I raved about it.

Christoph, of course, could no longer stand watching the film, I'd insisted on it so many times. But even he was impressed by the beauty of real-life Volterra, something no film or book could equal.

Hand in hand, we wandered through the narrow medieval alleys and the Porta all'Arco, the city gate dating back to Etruscan times. We admired the Palazzo dei Priori, the town's ancient palace. From time to time, Christoph would draw me close and kiss me passionately on one of the many overlooks that offered stunning views. How I wished we could stay longer.

Unfortunately, our trip neared its end far too soon, with only two days left for Florence—barely enough time to sample its treasures. Still, we kept our pace leisurely as we strolled through the medieval streets. I admired the old houses and let my fingers run over their rough Tuscan stone walls. I have always enjoyed touching surfaces, appreciating the feel of them—warm or cold, soft or hard—experiencing them with all my senses. It is the only way to really take in the surroundings and makes discovering something new so much more intense and exciting.

For our final stop, Christoph and I visited the famous cathedral, Santa Maria del Fiore. Up close, it seemed almost unreal, it was that powerful . . . that immense. We walked up all 414 steps to the campanile—yes, we counted them. We also climbed the narrow and steep stairs to the cupola, a strenuous undertaking. But once at the top, the dazzling views made us forget the painstaking ascent.

We'd waited in line a long time to get into the cathedral, so once we'd had our fill of the scenery, we called it quits.

The next day, the four of us indulged in an exquisite lunch before hitting the road back to Graz. Cherishing the memories of our trip already, I knew I could never have imagined a better way to celebrate my graduation.

Once we were home, Christoph dropped me off at my apartment. After carrying my bags upstairs, he leaned against the door frame with a smile on his face, his eyes tired from the long drive. Even so, he still looked incredibly handsome. I was so happy he was mine, and I knew I'd never want anyone else. Christoph was the love of my life. I knew it. Just knew it. Every time I saw him, I fell in love all over again, each time more deeply.

"Thank you for this amazing trip, Chris." I stood on tiptoe and wrapped my arms around his neck. His eyes shone into mine and then closed as I tenderly kissed his lips, a kiss which quickly turned passionate. His mouth opened, and his tongue tasted my own. He moaned with desire. I smiled, my lips against his, and then leaned back in his arms for a moment.

"Why don't you stay over tonight?" I murmured. I pulled him inside and closed the door behind us.

Chapter 1
Mia—Always the Same

Graz, March 2011

I was waiting for Christoph . . . again. His constant lateness was an issue we fought about over and over. This time, we were late for an important reception that my newspaper was hosting.

Pacing my hallway, all dressed up for the evening, I worried I would make a bad impression if I didn't get there on time, which would lead to teasing by my coworkers. Even though I'd been with the company for a year and a half, including my internship, I had been a full-time employee for only nine months, so my colleagues still treated me like the newbie.

If Christoph didn't hurry and get here soon, we could forget about going altogether. I would head out by myself next time. I was livid.

But I kept waiting. When the bell finally rang, I opened the door and glared at Christoph, my arms crossed over my chest. "Where on earth have you been? Can't you be on time just once?" I hissed.

I grabbed my purse and moved past him down the stairs. He slammed the door shut and hurried after me. When he caught up, I turned around and saw his expression was amused.

"I'm glad to see you think it's funny when I'm late because of you," I snapped and turned, prepared to stomp down the remaining stairs. Putting his hands on my shoulders and softly stroking them up and down, he stopped me.

But I was not in the mood. "Cut that out."

"Oh, come on, Mimi. I'm only . . ." He glanced at his watch.

"Yeah, exactly. You are only *thirty minutes* late, Chris. We'll get there like, super late, and my team was supposed to arrive early. This wouldn't happen if we lived together."

He sighed loudly, closed his eyes, and let go of my shoulders, massaging the bridge of his nose and letting his head drop back.

"Do we really need to discuss this now?" He hated having this conversation. Truth be told, so did I, but I wanted him to give me a reason instead of evading the topic every time. The silence lengthened, and I finally gave up thinking it would be this time.

Without looking at each other, we continued down the stairs. On the middle landing, I paused again. I couldn't let it go.

To steady myself, I inhaled and exhaled evenly, then turned to face him. "I'm sorry. But it *would* make everything easier," I said, my voice now calm.

Chris ran his fingers through his blond hair. "No, Mia. I . . . OK, let's have this conversation right now, this very moment." His hand furrowed through his hair again, and then, once more, he massaged his nose. His whole body was tense, his brown eyes wide.

He stepped to the left, the right, then finally stopped and looked directly at me, seeming much more composed. "Look . . . I'm sorry."

I still had my arms crossed. Gently, Christoph untangled them and tenderly grasped my hands in his. His thumbs caressed their backs.

"Look, Mimi, we're still young. We can move in together in a few years."

That was always his default answer. How long was I supposed to wait? I wasn't the most patient person to begin with, and we weren't *that* young. I was twenty-three and wanted to live with my boyfriend, who happened to be two years older. We had been dating for four years. What was there left to wait for?

I bit my lower lip. Why didn't he see how much easier everything would be if he moved in with me? Or I with him, although that didn't seem to be an option, either. I just couldn't understand what made him hesitate. After all, he kept telling me how much he loved me. Wasn't that reason enough to at least start thinking about living together? To make plans? We didn't even have to live in his or my apartment. We could look for a new one. Maybe something bigger.

But he wasn't having any of it. He released my hands and stroked his thumb over my mouth. "Stop chewing on your beautiful lips. You'll eventually destroy them," he whispered and gave me a sweet kiss.

I couldn't help it. I had to smile. Under his touch, my body relaxed. I could never hold on to any bitterness toward Christoph for too long.

"Please don't be upset. I'll be over at your place as often as possible."

His reassurances didn't satisfy me. Now that we were actually on the subject, I wanted to hear more than the usual excuses.

I chose my words carefully. "What I don't get is why you are against it. You almost live here anyway. We sleep in the same bed almost every night. You have so many clothes in my dresser that I'll have to buy a new one soon. Why don't you just give up your place? Or if you prefer, I wouldn't mind moving into your place. Or maybe we could rent a different apartment?"

"I don't know." He sighed. "Maybe I'm not ready yet for this step. OK? I . . . Mia, I don't know how to explain this." He spoke very quietly and tugged me closer so he could lean his forehead against mine. "Everything would feel so . . . permanent."

My eyes opened wide. *Permanent?* That was exactly what I wanted. But apparently he didn't. I slipped out of his embrace, backed up against the wall, and crossed my arms again.

"Oh, damn it, wrong word," he said, looking frustrated. "I know we're supposed to be *permanent*, but I don't know whether I can make this leap just now. I love being at your place. I like your apartment better than mine. It's always so clean and cozy."

In spite of myself, I smiled again.

Christoph came closer. "Mimi, I love being with you. You know that." He took a deep breath and exhaled, resting his shoulder against the wall beside me. "I'm just worried that once we live together for real that things will change between us. Maybe they won't stay as good as they are now. And I don't want anything to be different. I always want us to stay as good together as we have been."

So that's what was worrying him. I held his face between my hands and whispered against his lips. "Christoph, nothing will change. We won't allow things to change. OK?"

He looked at me warily and sighed again. "We will move in together. Eventually. I promise. Please give me some time . . ."

I could only nod and bite my lip again.

"Don't." He grinned and placed a kiss on the tip of my nose. "Let's go. Otherwise we'll really be late."

I poked his waist.

When we were together, I simply couldn't stay mad at him.

Chapter 2
Mia—The World Is Floating

Graz, April 2011

Since March, things had been getting worse. I felt disheartened, gloomy, as if all my energy had been sucked away and my batteries were dead. I was exhausted. I wanted to sleep all day.

Where had the good times gone? Nothing seemed to be working out. The fights with Christoph about our living situation had intensified. What was his problem with packing a few boxes and moving in with me? I still couldn't wrap my head around his stubbornness.

There's no understanding a guy's brain. Yet, the truth was having his things here wouldn't change anything. He literally spent every night at my place anyway. Why keep an apartment where you spend two hours a day, at most? It represented his tiny piece of freedom, I supposed. But didn't I give him enough space? He was free to do whatever he pleased—I didn't object when he wanted to go out by himself or pursue his hobbies. I valued my own time alone far too much to ever interfere with his need for privacy. But I did want to take the next step; I didn't like the sound of *eventually*.

Constant fatigue added to my slump. All I wanted to do was stay in bed, but I banished even the thought of sleep into a far corner of my mind. There was no time for sleep.

I worked hard at the newspaper because I wanted to move up and I wanted my coworkers to accept me as an equal, yet that acceptance was proving out of reach. I loved the job! It was awesome, and I had an amazing boss who seemed happy with my performance, but most of my colleagues were thoughtless and dismissive. They treated me like an assistant, ordering me to fetch coffee and dumping grunt work on my desk when, in fact, we had the same responsibilities.

I was partly to blame for this, though. When I'd started working there, wanting to impress them, I'd been too shy to say no when they'd asked for favors. I'd also been convinced they'd see how enthusiastic and reliable I was, how motivated and ambitious, and how I could handle anything and everything they wanted me do.

After I'd said yes once, they'd taken it for granted I'd continue saying yes to every request. It wasn't long before a flood of Post-it notes always littered my workspace. I was expected to take care of revisions or finish research that nobody else wanted to deal with. I managed it all by carting my workload home with me at the end of every day, until the only time left to myself was limited to my lunch break and a few hours of sleep—definitely not enough sleep.

What with the countless all-nighters, my head constantly throbbed. My body was warning me it couldn't take much more.

A simple "no" would have improved my situation. But did I want to say it?

I wasn't ready, not yet. Despite its drawbacks, I loved my job and didn't want to jeopardize it in any way. And I was also feeling compelled to make up for recent lost time.

Over the past several weeks, I'd frequently been sick, requiring six or seven days off. I couldn't remember another stretch in my life when I'd been absent so often. I'd never even missed a single day of school.

It helped that my boss, Mr. Walter, was flexible and compassionate. Partly because, after all, I still turned in excellent work. While at home, I labored on a laptop from my bed, and Mr. Walter had my assignments on his desk, without fail, by every deadline.

After one or two days at home, I'd swallow some Advil and head back to the office, not really giving myself a chance to fully recover. So much time in bed hadn't cured my fatigue, either. I figured I'd just have to plug away, that eventually it would pass.

One morning, I felt particularly exhausted. When the piercing sound of the alarm clock jolted me from sleep, I couldn't be bothered to turn it off, as I was all snug under my duvet. I wished I could just disappear beneath the covers, become invisible.

"Mimi, turn off that damned alarm already!" Chris groaned, still half-asleep.

Why didn't he turn it off himself? I started to reach, then stopped. My every movement was extremely painful, and it didn't help that he poked me with his elbow.

After a moment, he cursed under his breath. Then he heaved a sigh. "Don't bother. I'll do it," he said. The alarm clock was on my bedside table. Christoph rolled over, his full weight on top of me, and turned it off.

Get off me, get off me . . . I tried to shove him away. My god. I hurt.

But he didn't budge. He thought it was funny. I could feel his body shaking as he tried to suppress his laughter. I freed my hands and pulled the duvet from over my face.

"Christoph, please . . ." I begged, but his laughter grew louder, echoing in my throbbing head. "Please, get off me. You're crushing me!"

"Good morning to you, too, princess." He kissed my forehead and finally rolled away.

I didn't feel even a spark of good humor. My body was burning hot. My limbs ached. My head pounded. What could I do? My job awaited. I focused on the only thing that would keep me going, as it always did—knowledge that at the end of the day, I'd snuggle up in my warm and comfy bed next to Christoph, who'd arrive as usual after he got off work. Then I could forget about everything and fall asleep at his side. That was the light on my horizon, undimmed by the issue of whether we'd move in together or not.

But before I could reach that point, I had to make it through an entire long workday. What cheered me up somewhat was the prospect of lunch with Julia, once the morning was over.

Feeling crushed from just a few hours of work, I waited for my best friend in the small restaurant across the street from my office building. Carelessly, I threw my bag on the seat next to me, and a pen and compact tumbled out to the ground. Damn it. What once had been a mirrored compact was now just so much crumbled powder on the floor. I found a tissue in my purse and tried to clean up the mess.

"Hey, Mia. What are you up to under the table?"

I startled and hit my head on the wooden top. Ouch! As if I wasn't suffering enough already.

Rubbing my brow, I turned to Julia, knowing my face must be contorted with pain. "Just trying to look at the world from another perspective."

"And does it look better from down there?" Julia smiled.

"I guess, today, the world looks pretty much the same no matter the angle," I moaned. I expected my skull to explode any minute.

"Jeez, you look exhausted." Sliding onto the chair across from me, Julia studied me, her expression concerned.

I shrugged. I didn't want to worry anyone over a lousy headache. It wasn't a big deal . . . well, except when you added the pain in my limbs and the cramp in my right side. I just needed a few days of good sleep, and I would be back on my feet. Maybe Christoph and I could take a short vacation, do nothing. We hadn't been anywhere since our trip to Italy, and that was almost a year ago.

Julia's voice broke through my thoughts.

"Mia, have you lost weight?" She inspected as much of me as she could see over the table, then pointed to my chest. "You *have* lost weight. Your blouse is too big. What's going on?"

The waitress interrupted us. After we ordered, Julia reached across and took my hand. I could see the worry in her eyes. "Over the past several weeks, you've been sick a lot. That's not the Mia I know."

"Oh, it's nothing. This morning, I woke up with a headache. That's why I look tired. I'm fine." But was I really? Or was I only trying to convince myself?

Julia's eyes grew wide, and she shook her head. "Keep telling yourself that. Maybe it helps. Seriously, is everything OK?"

I ran a hand through my long, blond hair and nodded while trying to feign a smile. But the corners of my mouth wouldn't do what I wanted, and all I managed was a grimace.

"No worries, Julia. I'm just slammed with work." Nervous at her continuing scrutiny, I twirled a strand of hair between my fingers. "Man, I'm sick and tired of being the newbie. I've been there for a year and a half. When will they get that?"

"They still haven't accepted you? I can't believe it. Show them what you're capable of," Julia said.

I took a deep breath. "That's what I'm trying to do. It's why I'm working so hard. And they still make me the gofer. But it'll get better. I hope. At least I want for it to get better."

She smiled but looked skeptical. "Listen Mia," she whispered. "Here's a little secret for you. Just say no."

"All right, I hear you. I'll learn to. Eventually." Playfully, I kicked her shin under the table.

"Hey! Just saying." She giggled. "Seriously. You have to make sure work doesn't get to be too much for you."

I nodded and bit my lower lip. "It won't. Like I've said before, we're all under the gun."

My remark—or was it an excuse?—didn't seem to convince her. "I understand you have a lot on your plate right now. Same here. But you don't look healthy. I've never seen such dark circles under your eyes. Even after a weekend of all-nighters. Are you sure everything is OK?"

"Julia, please . . ." I looked at her, imploring her to let it drop. "Everything is fine. I swear."

She nodded and finally let it go. But I knew she'd bring it up again. Today, though, I'd had enough of her motherly attitude. This lunch break was supposed to distract me from work and pain, not force me to focus on it.

After lunch with Julia, the afternoon dragged. Finally, I could hurry home and hide under my covers. Five minutes after I'd climbed into bed, Christoph arrived. A few days before, I had made him a copy of my keys in an attempt to make this seem like his home. When I'd presented the chain, he'd taken it without hesitation, and I'd even seen a faint smile on his face.

He sat down beside me, leaned over, and hugged me. I was so glad to feel his arms around me.

"I've missed you all day," I whispered. "I haven't been feeling well, and all I want is to relax next to you."

He smiled. "Well, that won't be too hard to manage," he said, kicking off his shoes and slipping under the covers.

· · ·

Another week went by, and I was still finding it difficult to get up in the mornings. But I didn't stay home. I was worried Mr. Walter wouldn't be lenient forever, and I didn't want to risk getting fired.

I just had to suck it up. The weekend was in sight, only two more days to go. I would not take work home with me this time. I would turn off my cell phone, disconnect the Internet, and hole up in my apartment. All I needed to feel better was a few days alone with Christoph.

But that day, I had to work until seven. I slouched out of the office. My body felt sluggish, drained of every tiny bit of energy. On my way home, I could hardly keep my eyes open. Fortunately, I was only a few houses away. Inside, I practically crawled up the three flights of stairs. Every step felt like torture. The cramping in my side had grown more intense. I wished I could simply lie down right there, fall asleep on the cool floor, and never get up again.

Somehow I reached my door. My hand shook as I searched my purse for the key, then tried to insert it into the lock. The stupid thing wouldn't go, but fortunately, that didn't matter. Christoph opened the door from inside.

"Where have you been?" Reaching out, Christoph placed one hand behind my back, steered me into the apartment, then closed the door behind me.

I leaned against him heavily and slurred a response that was supposed to be "at work" but sounded more like "awerk." I was moving my lips, but the sounds didn't make sense. It was like my brain had been cut off from my mouth.

Slowly, Christoph turned me around to face him. His brown eyes looked scared.

"Mimi? Are you OK?" He cupped my face. "You're burning hot."

I'm OK, Chris...

"Mimi? Mia... Mia! Come on, say something." There was so much fear on his face. Why was he so afraid?

I'm here, I'm OK.

"Mimi, please look at me." I could feel his arms holding me up. His heart beat wildly against my chest. His breath was fast.

I was calm. Unlike his, my heart beat steadily. I felt safe in his embrace. I felt good. I felt as if I were floating.

"Mimi, stay with me. Stay with me!"

I was floating . . .

Chapter 3
Mia—Fear

Graz, June 2012

"Mia, do you really have to go through with this?"

"Yes, Mom." Irritated, I tossed the clothes I'd been holding onto my bed.

My hands clenched. I looked down and forced myself to take ten even breaths. My heart rate slowed. I stretched, clenching and unclenching my fingers until I managed to breathe normally and was composed again.

I couldn't stand it when this happened. I still hadn't regained complete control over my body or my emotions. I particularly hated it when it happened in front of my parents. They had already suffered more than enough for me. They didn't need my tantrums and emotional chaos on top of everything else. Warily, I glanced at my mother, then took another ten breaths. Finally, I was able to speak without animosity and anger in my voice.

"I need distance." With both arms, I gestured around the room. "Distance from everything. I know, or at least I think I know, that this is for the best. Please try to understand that," I implored.

She looked at me, her green eyes showing so many emotions—grief, fear, compassion, care—all because of her daughter. I looked away. I didn't want to see her sorrow.

She and my dad had tried to persuade me not to go on this trip. Especially my mom. My dad had given up after only a short while. He knew I would leave, no matter what they said. After all, I had inherited his stubbornness. Once I'd made up my mind, it was like talking to a wall.

In certain situations, this stubbornness was a blessing. It helped me reach my goals. It was the reason I had finished my studies in no time and with straight As. It had led me into the perfect job.

But in other situations, the obstinacy was counterproductive.

It was partly to blame for my sadness, which was a considerable obstacle. How could I move past it? Was I capable of eliminating what stood in my way? Maybe the solution to coming to terms with my future lay in my stubbornness. Yet I had no clue where to even begin looking for myself.

And I wasn't sure whether something that I'd soon lose forever anyway would be worth searching for, worth any struggle at all.

Yet I had set my mind to make this trip. I simply had to do it. I needed time. Time for myself. Time away from everything that made me so bitchy and bitter. The self I had become was a stranger to me, and I didn't like that stranger. I wanted her to disappear. But she wouldn't. Each new day seemed to bring a fight that I was bound to lose.

I sighed and walked over to my mom. I looked at her for a long time. She didn't move. Clumsily, I hugged her.

The way forward was going to be difficult for all of us.

I was scared.

I was afraid to be alone after what had happened during the past year.

I was afraid of what this new life would look like.

I was afraid I wouldn't find my way back to my real self.

I was afraid of what would happen should I find it.

I was afraid I would never find it and never come back.

"I'm so sorry, Mom," I murmured, my lips pressed against her hair.

"Ah, Mia . . ." She pulled me closer. "Take care of yourself. Promise to be in touch as often as you can."

I promised I would. Definitely.

I knew my parents were worried. They were scared, concerned I was still too fragile to travel.

I understood. I wasn't sure I had the stamina, either. No clue at all, to be precise. But if I didn't try, I would never know. I just had to go.

It would be only one month. One month across Europe by train. Alone. Just me and myself. It was time to get out of here.

My mother loosened her embrace and stroked my hair. The short, thin hair on my head.

Instantly, I flinched, and my heartbeat accelerated. My whole body went on red alert. I didn't like anyone to touch me there. I hated my scalp. What adorned it now reminded me of a baby's fuzz. Fine, thin, no style. Away from home, I hid my head under a knitted hat, which I took off only when I was here, so only my parents knew how I really looked. I'd learned that with the hat off, people stared. I always eluded their gazes. They made me feel naked. True, some people looked at me with compassion, but I didn't want them to look at me at all. Even I couldn't stand to look at myself, so why should strangers catch even a glimpse? My preferred option would have been to dissolve into invisibility, but unfortunately, things didn't work like that.

I missed my old life and my long hair—flaxen, like my mom's. Friends had often told me how they envied my golden mane. Well, now there was nothing left to envy.

Now I was the one who felt envy. Or who would have felt envy, had there been any friends around. But there weren't any. One after the other had moved on, which didn't make things easier.

I missed a shoulder to lean on. I longed for someone outside my family who would support me. I missed warmth and laughter.

I'm sure it had been difficult to be around me during those months, but I always assumed people I loved, who claimed to love me, would stick with me. Apparently, I had it all wrong.

Situations like mine teach you who your real friends are. I'd never imagined nobody would stand by me. We'd experienced so many things together, but none of those times with each other seemed to count, except to me.

I wouldn't have abandoned them. I wouldn't have let them down.

But what had happened to me . . .

It was too much for them. It was too much for me.

And it was too much for Christoph . . .

Chapter 3 ½
Mia—You Can't Heal While You're in Pain

Graz, August 2011

The day had started out a good one. I had even managed the steps, a rare feat over the past few weeks. Everyone wanted me downstairs more often. They tried to boost my morale. But they had no clue how I felt and what I was really going through.

How I hated that question: "How are you today?"

Fantastic, thank you. Guess I never felt better.

They should stop asking. All of them. I didn't answer anyway, so what was the point?

Yet that particular day had been good. Maybe it was the silence. Nobody was home to pepper me with questions or fill the stillness with chatter. The mornings had become my favorite time of day. The house was empty and quiet. The only sound came from the ticking of the pendulum clock.

My parents were at work. They'd needed their daily routine back. I understood; I missed mine. Without it, I was just a pain in everyone's neck, including my own.

I was sick and tired of sitting in my room hour after hour, with nothing to occupy my time, nothing for me to do in this house—nothing I enjoyed, anyway. By then, most of my so-called friends had disappeared. Christoph was my one silver lining in this whole ordeal, but we didn't do much else besides sit next to each other, watch TV, or talk. Except for talking, of course, which I no longer cared for, I could do the rest by myself. Yet his presence reassured me. He gave me strength and was the reason I fought a little harder each day. I fought for him—and for us.

That day he had promised to take off work. The prospect of having him around for more than just a few hours cheered me up.

As always, he was running behind. I'd been sitting in the kitchen for over an hour and was growing worried. I knew he was never on time, but usually he wasn't more than a half hour late.

I tapped in his number on my cell phone.

"Hey, where are you? I've been waiting forever," I said.

"Hey, Mia. Um . . . I . . ."

Something was off. He was never at a loss for words. He seemed nervous.

"Are you all right, Chris?"

He didn't answer. I only heard him breathe.

"Chris, please, say something. You sound confused. Is everything OK?" I repeated.

The silence grew longer, scaring me. This behavior wasn't normal. I tried to remain patient, never my forte. I wanted everything to happen fast. Time was important to me. I needed time. And yet I waited.

"Mia, I . . ." I heard a ragged inhale. I didn't need to see him to know he was running his left hand through his hair, his default gesture when he was nervous.

"OK, well . . . Mia . . . I can't do this any longer. I can't deal with it."

A huge knot gripped my stomach. I must have misheard. Lately, it seemed I couldn't trust my own senses. Reality and dreams often merged. This must be a dream. A nightmare.

"This isn't working anymore, Mia. Every day I see you suffer, and I don't know what to do. I can't help you." Christoph sighed.

I was frozen. I didn't know what to say.

"It hurts me to see you in such pain," he added sadly. I could barely hear his voice.

"Chris . . ." I got up from my chair and began pacing. Growing short of breath in moments, I gripped the countertop to steady myself. My knees shook; my entire body trembled.

This *was* a nightmare.

No, it wasn't. It was real.

"What are you doing?" I whispered. In anticipation of what was coming, I turned around and leaned back against the cupboards. "You are . . . Does that mean you are really . . . ? No, Chris, no!" My heart was about to burst. I couldn't breathe. I felt as if I were choking.

"I'm so very sorry, Mia, but I can't go on like this."

We both fell silent. For five endless minutes, neither of us said a word. We only listened to the sounds of our breathing.

"I'm terribly sorry. Really, I am so, so sorry," he murmured. His voice was barely audible.

It was true.

I wasn't about to just take this in stride. "Seriously?" I snapped. "You've got to be kidding me. How do you think I feel? I am fighting for myself every goddamn day!" My brain had finally processed his words, I'd realized the full impact of what was happening, and I couldn't hold back the tears any longer. They began streaming down my face. I hurt so bad . . .

"Chris, do you have any idea what I'm dealing with? I don't know what to do to feel better. And you're just thinking of yourself? How *you* feel?" A seemingly endless cascade of tears ran down my cheeks.

So much for my good day.

The situation was almost too much to bear. My knees started to buckle, even though I pressed my back harder against the countertop, hoping to somehow stay on my feet. The tears continued to fall.

"Don't be so selfish, Mia." His voice startled me, not much louder than a whisper and far too calm. He continued, "This is also about me."

I shook my head. This had to be a bad dream. Could I please wake up and continue my life where I'd left it? Any moment now, surely I would. That's how things worked, didn't they?

My headache returned with violent force. One hand gripping the counter to keep me upright, I used the other to massage my temples, trying to keep the pain at bay. I let my fingers trail through what was left of my hair.

"Selfish?" I said quietly. "You're calling me selfish . . . ?" My voice grew louder. "Yeah, right, I chose this situation. Upon every falling star I saw, I wished 'Oh please, choose me. I love to suffer. I am so young. Take me! And don't just ruin a few years—no, please ruin my whole goddamn life.' Yeah, Christoph, that's how selfish I am."

My heart beat furiously. My entire body was in pain.

"I am so sorry." That's all he seemed able to say. I didn't believe him. The silence between us returned. A very uncomfortable silence, broken only by some muted sounds in the background. And then I heard a voice. A very familiar, female voice.

"Chris, babe, come back to bed, will you?"

I was speechless. What was there to say, anyway?

Christoph and my *best friend*.

Breathing was suddenly difficult. It was as if someone was choking me. Hoarsely, I asked, "Since when?"

"Mimi . . ."

"Don't *Mimi* me!" I hissed. *Mimi*—his nickname for me. Only I wasn't his Mimi anymore. I didn't even want to be his Mimi anymore.

"It's not what you think it is."

"Not what I think it is? Then what is it? Seems pretty obvious to me!"

"It just happened. You were never around, always in the hospital, and Julia and I often got together to talk about you. All the time; I only thought about you."

He paused, waiting for me to say something, but I was out of words. God, this hurt.

"We always talked about how we could help you. Then one night she was at my door, crying. She and Hofi had been fighting. And then . . . it just happened. Some things you can't control. They just happen." I heard him swallow. "She's breaking up with Markus."

Some things just happen.

"I get it, Christoph. I'm selfish, and some things just happen. I've heard enough!" I yelled and hung up.

I smashed my cell phone against the wall. It broke into little pieces. It wasn't the only thing broken. The pain in my heart was excruciating. I'd never imagined Chris could do this to me. I'd been convinced his love for me was as strong as my love for him. And I'd been so wrong.

I wanted to end it all. I sobbed and screamed and threw everything I could find to the floor—plates, glasses, silverware—until I was exhausted and had no strength left in my body. My knees gave, and I fell to the hard tiles on the floor.

Not what I think it is.

Chapter 4
Mia—I Can Do That

Graz, June 2012

My mother was fearful I wasn't ready to go on the trip. That I wasn't healthy enough. I had my doubts, too. Like her, I didn't know whether I'd regained enough strength.

Over the past year, my parents had witnessed all my ups and downs. If I were in her shoes, I would have been just as troubled. She had seen me at my worst. There had been days when I'd locked myself in my room—well, Anna's room. After I'd moved out, my younger sister had inherited my bedroom, neither of us ever imagining I'd be back. But then, at age twenty-four and a half, I'd ended up unable to care for myself, my only solution to move back in with my parents.

There had been days I'd been so defeated by self-doubt and anxiety that I couldn't swallow a single bite. I'd been so weak and lacked the courage to face my future. I hadn't wanted to go on living.

I'd felt like a loser, a total failure in life. I'd wondered how I could ever get my feet under me again.

My parents had tried everything to help me see the beauty that still surrounded me. In an attempt to remind me of the things I'd loved, they'd bought me a new set of drawing pencils.

I had always enjoyed sketching, especially with chalk or monolith pencils. With them, I'd rendered drawings that mirrored events in my life. But I'd no longer wanted to even talk about my emotions, let alone depict them. I gave art up. I locked up my talent deep inside my heart and left the sketching pencils in the desk drawer.

My parents had done and still did everything they could to cheer me up and welcome me back into a daily routine. Every time my mom cooked dinner, she called me to join her in the kitchen. She knew how I'd loved cooking aromas, how I'd enjoyed peering over her shoulder to learn new culinary tricks. But not anymore. It was plain torture.

I simply had no energy to pick up the pieces. My body was exhausted, my inner life annihilated. I felt worthless. But I had to move on, somehow . . . if not for me, then for the sake of my family.

The pain had slowly done me in. I'd been desperate, so I'd tried to numb my suffering by intentionally harming myself. I'd hid the scars I'd inflicted under long sleeves. I hadn't known how else to handle my overwhelming emotions.

It had helped. That precise moment when the blade cut into the skin and the pain overpowered all the other aches in my body. At least briefly. For one fleeting moment, short as the blink of an eye.

But I felt better now . . .

My mother looked at me with sadness.

I had to be resolute. "Mom, I can do this." I smiled at her. I knew I could.

"I know. I know," she sighed. "I just worry so much about you. You're my child. Parents always worry about their children."

She had a point there. She still cautioned me to drive carefully every time I took the car.

"It's been such a difficult year for you. All I want is for you to enjoy your life. I want the best for you," she said softly and gently caressed my cheek.

That touch is allowed. She is my mother.

Then she straightened her shoulders. "Come on, let's not talk about this right now. This should be a joyful day. Especially for me. Finally, I'll have one less daughter in the house. The two of you together are driving me crazy."

"Mom!"

She shrugged. "It's true, Mia. One of you is always in the bathroom. I'm a woman, too, and I'd like my turn from time to time. Especially in the mornings, before going to work. But soon, I'll have one less person to argue with."

I shook my head. "Mom, you're exaggerating."

"As if you knew. But no matter. Now, let's put your clothes into your backpack." She looked about with wide eyes. "Seriously, you want to take all of this?"

She grasped my arm, and reluctantly, I let her drag me closer to the big, jumbled pile of stuff. But I wasn't really paying attention. My thoughts had wandered back in time again.

Chapter 4 ½
Mia—Bits and Pieces of My Life

Graz, September 2011

I didn't know what to do with myself. Day in and day out, I paced through a big, empty house. Most of the week, my parents were at work, and my little sister was at school. Anna was leading the good life: A happy life with friends, free from gnawing pain and crushing worries. Nothing serious, no life-threatening changes weighed her down.

My own life consisted of little except hospitalizations, nausea, and devastating, existential fears.

My soul suffered. Emptiness and rage consumed me.

I hated everything. I didn't understand why fate had been so cruel. Fury made me do things I'd never thought I was capable of.

One day, I'd been particularly angry. In the morning, I'd talked on the phone with Christoph. I despised myself for still answering his calls, but I couldn't seem to stop. I was still attached to him. I hated him because he had broken up with me, but at the same time, I still loved him. And Christoph? Well, apparently, he couldn't let go, either.

He probably had a guilty conscience prompting him to call me every day. He said he wanted to make sure I was doing OK.

Those conversations never failed to stir up my emotions. I'd end up furious at myself for not staying strong, not ignoring his calls. Every time my cell rang, I checked the name on the display, and when it was his, I answered. And then questioned my sanity. I had to be out of my mind in order to still put up with him. In his sweetest voice, he'd call me Mimi, and then I'd fall for him all over. It was especially ridiculous because Julia hadn't broken up with Markus after all, and her affair with Christoph had remained just that, an affair. But Christoph couldn't win me back, ever, even if I often felt on the verge of returning to him.

That day, I was livid I'd once again not managed to tell him to go to hell.

I wanted to rid myself of everything. Of hospitalizations, of infuriating ex-boyfriends. All I'd cared about had gone down the drain. Nothing had worked out. Whatever I'd started had ended in chaos.

I wanted to die. Why did fate keep me alive? To wake up to the same torture and self-doubt every morning? That was not life.

I wanted to escape my thoughts. Was there no way of silencing them?

Why me? Nobody likes me now. I don't like myself. Look at me. Look at what I've become. No hair, only skin and bones. I look sick. Nobody wants to deal with sick people. Everyone has disappeared from my life. Maybe I should disappear, as well.

Moving to the bathroom, then standing in front of the large mirror, I examined myself from head to toe. Ugly. It was the only word that sprang to mind.

Suddenly I broke. Over and over again, I pounded against my reflected image while tears streamed down my face. I screamed, "Get out of my face! Get out of my life! I hate you. Go away!"

I punched the mirror so fiercely that it shattered. Shards scattered around my feet. Blood dripped from slashes along my fingers and knuckles. I stared at my hands, turning them back and forth, then focused on the crimson droplets dotting the mirror fragments on the floor.

I sat down and listened to the steady rhythm of my heartbeat. I picked up the biggest chunk of glass and inspected it carefully. It was razor-sharp, sharp enough to terminate this misery, to bring the end I so desperately wanted.

I sucked in a deep breath and placed the jagged edge on my lower left arm. I pressed it deep into my skin until the pain grew nearly unbearable. Until the pain overwhelmed every other hurt.

Riveted by what I'd done, I stared at the blood running down my wrist, dripping onto the floor. My right hand clasped the shard tighter as I guided it once again to my flesh. Slowly, I drew it upward. The open wound grew.

My pulse was slow and steady. I wasn't afraid anymore. This was what I wanted. The end.

"Mia, no! Stop!"

At the boom of my father's voice, I dropped the shard.

Terrified, I looked first at him, then at the huge gash I'd self-inflicted. A puddle of blood had formed around my feet. My clothes were streaked crimson. And there I was: an impassive and motionless observer.

"Mia, press this against the cut!" My dad shoved a towel at me and lifted me from the floor.

"Bear down!" he ordered, grabbing my right hand to guide it to the towel. He hoisted me in his arms, then carried me through the door, down the stairs, and into his car. "You keep pressing down on the wound. You understand me?" As we sped through the late-afternoon rush hour, he whispered, "Why?"

I didn't answer. All I could do was stare out the window and then at my arm. The white towel grew redder with every minute. It fascinated me, watching each fiber of the fabric turn scarlet.

Some drops fell onto my jeans. I didn't press on the wound. Nothing hurt. And I wanted this injury to end it all.

The car stopped. My dad ran around the car, dragging me from the passenger seat into the ER. After he screamed for help, far too many people surrounded me. An orderly—a nurse?—hustled me into a small room, placed me on a gurney, and inspected my arm, turning it to look at one side, then the other while compressing the wound.

I felt so light and free as I observed the turmoil from a distance. A doctor entered. He cleaned the wound and stitched it, and while he labored over me, he asked why. I didn't answer. Before I left the hospital, it would seem everyone there had asked me that same stupid question. Wasn't it obvious? Who needed an answer?

I lay motionless on the gurney, like a stone, and stared at the white neon lights on the ceiling. I asked myself again, *Why me?* If my father hadn't returned home earlier than usual, my misery would be over.

Chapter 5
Mia—My Sunshine

Graz, June 2012

"Mia, is everything all right?" My mother's voice brought me back to the present. I was still alive. And I was feeling better. A year ago, all I could think about was that one question: Why me? Now I wasn't as obsessed with it anymore. Suppressing things was supposed to help, wasn't it?

"Yes, Mom. I just . . . Whatever. Let's just keep going." I touched the long scar on my arm and turned back to my backpack.

My pack was spacious, but I really had chosen too many things to take.

My mother stared at the pile on my bed. "We'll never find room for all these clothes. What do you need these shoes for?" She dangled a pair of beloved high heels between her fingers. "You haven't worn them in a year, and now you want to take them on a train trip? I must have done something terribly wrong when I raised you." She sighed loudly.

"Mom . . ." I scolded her and grabbed my shoes.

"Come on, Mia. It was just a joke." She smiled at me. "Though, seriously, you should leave them here." She circled an arm around my waist and rested her head on my shoulder. It was only a light caress. I didn't really like her touch, but this was my mom, and I knew she needed this closeness now.

She pressed a little closer, and I let her. She was the only person whose presence I could stand for longer than a few minutes. Not only was she my mother, she was also my best friend and one of the most beautiful women I knew. She really didn't show her fifty years. Maybe it was because of her long blond hair and big green eyes or her high cheekbones and full lips. She was so pretty.

I could understand why my father had fallen in love with her so many years ago. She simply made you smile. Her cheerfulness was contagious. She was my sun, the center of our small family.

"I will miss you, my big girl." She drew me even closer.

Slowly, I rubbed her back and then whispered, "I'll miss you, too. I really will . . ." I felt the shoulder of my shirt growing damp. Mom was crying.

Seeing her hurt was painful. Knowing I was the reason pained me even more. In moments like this, I considered abandoning my plan in order to make her feel better. But that was not an option.

"Mom, everything will be OK. I will be in touch." A sigh escaped my throat. "Maybe I'll be back soon," I added so quietly it was almost inaudible. I loosened my grip to look her in the eyes. When I kissed her cheek, I tasted the salt from her tears. "Also, I remember someone saying she was looking forward to having less women fighting over the bathroom."

She smiled as a few last tears trailed down her face. "I will miss you anyway," she said softly and stroked my cheek with the back of her hand. "Please take good care of yourself, will you, Mia? Promise you will come home if anything happens. Please."

So as not to cry, I nodded and bit my lower lip so hard that I tasted blood. The pain distracted me. For the sake of my family, I had to be strong. And I had to be strong for my own sake, as well.

"My beautiful girl." She smiled at me.

She always insisted that, with my green eyes and blond hair, I'd inherited her looks. But I'd never thought I matched her beauty, and right now, I clearly didn't.

My eyes were still green, but they looked dead, bruised from all the sleepless nights. My cheeks were hollow.

Not to mention my hair . . .

Chapter 5 ½
Mia—So Who am I?

Graz, June 2011

For the first time in a long time I'd gotten a good night's sleep. A night without tossing and turning. I wasn't awake at dawn to listen to the twittering birds. I'd slept straight through their morning chorus.

I yawned and stretched my aching limbs, then massaged my face and rubbed my eyes. As I sat up slowly, I ran my fingers through my long blond hair.

I froze. I must be dreaming. *Please don't let this be true.* My heart began to race, and my hands shook. I closed my eyes and lowered my hands to my lap.

Chewing my lower lip, I inhaled deeply and evenly through my nose. Hesitantly, I opened my eyes.

"No!" I let out a loud scream. Tears shot to my eyes.

Someone shouted my name. My sister rushed into my room and stopped, a panicked look on her face. I stared back at her with a blank expression.

"Mia, what's the matter?"

I continued to stare at her, my eyes wide. I could hardly breathe.

"Mia?" she asked gently.

I only shook my head.

Anna came closer.

"Anna? Am I dreaming? Please tell me I'm dreaming," I moaned.

Anna kneeled beside my bed and took the clump of hair I was holding. "No, Mia. I'm sorry, but this isn't a dream." I could hear the effort she made to keep her voice calm.

From that day on, I discovered hair on my pillow each morning. I suffered panic attacks. I screamed when I woke up. Whoever came into the room—whether my mother, my father, or my sister—had to calm me down and remind me to breathe.

I didn't want to comb my hair anymore or run my fingers through what once had been a great, thick mane. I was afraid I'd find more strands in the brush than were left on my head. Every day, my mother tried to soothe me when I went to her in tears, to show her yet another clump.

"My big girl, it's only hair. It will grow back again," she promised.

That was easily said, but nobody could imagine how I felt, losing it all.

I'd loved my long hair. Ever since I was a little girl, I'd let it grow. Hair is part of our personality, giving us confidence, defining who we are. It was a part of me.

And as my hair grew thinner, so did my self-worth.

Eventually, I was incapable of witnessing the gradual loss. Once I had only feathers left on my head, I shaved off what remained with my father's razor. All done, I was bald.

I stared for hours into the mirror at the stranger staring back, the empty shell of who I'd been. I was chalk white, with dark circles under my eyes. Each day, I'd grown thinner. Pricks and bruises from needle insertions covered my arms.

I couldn't stand to look at myself. I didn't know the person reflected back at me. She was a stranger. A stranger with my face. She looked like me, but she wasn't me.

Where was I supposed to search for the woman I'd once been? Did she still even exist?

How could I accept me when I hated myself?

Everything I saw in the mirror appalled me.

Chapter 6
Mia—A Long Good-bye

Graz, June 2012

The day of my departure finally arrived. I was nervous but still determined to go.

The train station was packed. People yelled from all directions, kissed loved ones good-bye, shed a few tears.

Standing on the platform, my mother and I hugged for a long time. The harried crowd swirled around us. Trains arrived and departed. But for mom and me, time stood still, and we savored this moment as best as we could.

I would miss her terribly. Throughout the past year, she had always been there for me, had worked to build up my shattered confidence.

I was so very grateful for all the support she'd given me while I'd undergone chemo and the unceasing onslaught of exams and checkups. For each appointment, she'd driven me to the hospital, waited half the day, then taken me home. She'd been my rock. She'd never complained, not even when I'd yelled at her out of rage at having to continue on.

I'd wanted her to leave me alone and let me rot. Sometimes I'd even drummed my fists against her. She'd only waited until I'd calmed down, until I'd collapse, sobbing in her arms.

She was everything to me. And I hadn't once thanked her.

She slowly released me from her embrace but didn't let go of my hands. She sucked in air, then gradually blew it out, her eyes shimmering. A faint smile played on her lips.

I glanced at my father; he'd been watching us and now gave me a sad nod. He wasn't one to display his emotions and preferred to keep a distance.

I took a deep breath and locked gazes with my mother. I bit my lower lip. It was hard for me, as well, to show my feelings or talk about them. In that way, I was like my father.

By now, Mom's eyes brimmed with tears. One lonely drop escaped, ran down her cheek, and fell to the ground. With both her hands, she caressed my upper arms. She wanted to make me feel relaxed, but I couldn't bear to see the pain in her eyes any longer and looked down.

"Thank you," I murmured, my eyes on the ground.

With an index finger, my mother tilted up my chin. "Look at me, Mia." She smiled and waited.

"Thank you, Mom. You've been there for me the whole year. Thank you for everything you did."

Another tear trailed down her cheek.

"I know I haven't been easy to deal with," I said very quietly. "But you never complained. Not once."

I lowered my gaze again. The sight of my mother, overwhelmed by her feelings and with tears coursing down her face, was too much for me to bear. But I needed her to know how much I loved her.

"I'm so grateful for you, for how you supported me in every situation. You've been the best mother, and the very best friend, anyone could ever have through an ordeal like this." Slowly I raised my eyes. "Thank you."

Mom threw her arms around me, and I had to make an effort to tolerate the sudden, intense physical contact.

Pressing her wet cheek against my neck, she sighed, "Ah, Mia, I'll always be here for you . . . always." She loosened her grip to better look at me. Across her tear-streaked face, I saw smudgy traces of her black mascara. She stood on tiptoe and whispered in my ear, "Take good care of yourself. Give us a call once you get there."

She hesitated but finally let go of me, smiling through her tears. I reached into my purse for a handkerchief, then handed it to her.

Clearing his throat, my father moved closer, patted my shoulder, and gave me a smile.

"You'll do this thing, Mia." He fought to keep his voice neutral, but in this situation like this, even my dad seemed to be finding it impossible to control his feelings.

"All I ask is for you to get back home safe and sound. Everything will be all right," he murmured.

My heart grew heavy when he mentioned my eventual return, but I didn't want to ruin the moment and remained silent.

My father took a step closer and did something I'd never have expected of him. He gave me a hug. A real hug. It felt weird and clumsy, but I liked it. It took me back to a time when I was ten and had hurt my knee. Crying, I had run to my dad and sobbed into the crook of his arm. He'd wiped my tears with his thumb, kissed my cheeks, and whispered that everything would be OK.

"Thank you, Dad . . ." I smiled and blinked rapidly. "Thank you for everything," I whispered, leaning my head against his chest. I felt so sheltered, I didn't even mind the physical contact.

"Be careful, my girl."

To hold back the tears, all I could do was nod. If I cried, I might have decided to stay, just to remain in the safe presence of my parents and my sister.

No. Under no circumstances. I had to be strong and stick to my plan.

Then Anna kissed me good-bye, and I boarded the train. There was no going back. This was supposed to be the *trip of my life*.

Slowly, the train began to move. I looked out the window one last time. My father was holding my mother, who was weeping against his shoulder. Dad's fingers caressed her arm. It hurt so much to see them like this.

I closed my eyes to compose myself. Then I looked back, feeling a bittersweet nostalgia. I forced a smile and waved good-bye to my parents and my sister.

I waved good-bye to my past.

I had to let go. I would miss them, although not my former life. Except for my family, I hated everything about it, including myself. Why should I hold on to an existence that had been destroyed in a single blow?

Chapter 6 ½
Mia—Nobody Wants to Hear That

Graz, April 2011

I don't think I'd ever experienced a day like this before.

For a week now, I had been in the hospital. My condition stressed me out, made me restless and irritated. I knew the drugs, treatments, exams, diet, and rest were all supposed to be for my benefit, but I was confined to bed and only allowed to get up when I really had to. My body was extremely weak. At least the high fever was dropping—raising my hopes for an early release, despite less-than-encouraging results from my blood work. For the time being, I was just glad I had a room all to myself.

The days dragged. My only comfort came on afternoons when Christoph visited. He always tried to cheer me up.

"Just wait and see, Mimi. You'll be out of here in no time. The results from the CT should be here any day now. I'm sure everything will be fine."

I sat up and looked at him warily. He took my hand in one of his, and with his other, he caressed my cheek. Then he kissed my lips.

"Don't worry. You were just overworked. These tests are routine. A mere formality."

I nodded and bit my lower lip. A CT didn't seem routine. My stomachaches had become so bad they were unbearable without painkillers, which was why they were doing further testing. The initial ultrasound hadn't revealed anything wrong.

With his thumb, he touched my mouth. "Don't. You will ruin your pretty lips," he said with a smile. Immediately, I stopped biting and smiled at him. "There's my beautiful Mia."

After awhile, we heard a knock on the door, and Dr. Ludwig and Dr. Oberbichler entered. Instantly my heart began to race. This was the moment I would hear the results.

Full of hope, I looked into the doctors' faces to see whether I could find an answer there, but they didn't reveal anything.

"Good afternoon, Frau Lang. We'd like to discuss some things with you." Dr. Oberbichler looked at Christoph. "We need to ask you to wait outside, please."

Christoph nodded and was about to get up, but I grabbed his hand. "Please, can't he stay?" I pleaded.

Both doctors looked at me with sympathy. Dr. Oberbichler inhaled deeply. "All right. Why not? You will probably need his support anyway."

Support? Why would I need support?

That didn't sound good. That did not sound good at all.

My heart pounded faster, and my hands trembled. Cold sweat broke out on my forehead, and of course I chewed on my lower lip again.

The doctors pulled chairs next to my bed, sat down, clipboards in hand, and exchanged glances heavy with meaning.

I stared at them. Neither spoke. How much longer would they delay this?

In sheer desperation, I gripped Christoph's hand tighter. He squeezed back, then reached with his other to stroke my hair before leaning forward to lightly kiss my forehead.

Finally, the doctors looked directly at me. The younger one, Dr. Ludwig, rose and moved closer.

"Would you please remove your gown for another brief examination?"

I nodded and hastily pulled the hospital gown over my head.

Dr. Ludwig pressed his fingers against my right armpit and side. With an instrument that resembled a magnifying glass, he inspected an area. When he finished, I donned the gown again. He sat down and nodded to his colleague.

Both of them looked me straight in the eyes. Dr. Ludwig said, "We won't beat around the bush, Frau Lang. I wish we had better news, but the test results indicate a serious situation."

I glanced at Christoph, whose former smile had turned into a grimace. Slowly, I turned back to Dr. Ludwig.

He continued, "The CT clearly shows a lump on your liver and another under your armpit."

Chris's clasp on my hand was almost painful. From the corner of my eye, I could see him now staring at me, terrified. But I couldn't face him. I kept my gaze on the two doctors. My pulse raced. My hands were wet with sweat. What did this all mean?

"Frau Lang, we need to biopsy and likely excise those areas. As soon as your fever drops, we highly recommend surgery."

I nodded slowly. I couldn't speak. My brain tried to interpret the information it had just received. So much for not beating around the bush! Everything sounded confusing.

For a brief moment, silence reigned. Then Christoph broke it with frantic questions.

"What does that mean? *Lump?*"

"It means tumor," Dr. Ludwig answered.

With a trembling voice, I asked, "Tumors? I have . . . I have cancer?" Now it was Dr. Oberbichler's turn. He sat on my bedside. "Frau Lang, we have discovered a melanoma under your armpit."

I stared at him without moving. My heart rate normalized. My brain didn't understand what was going on.

"We suspect you have stage three skin cancer."

Christoph jumped up so violently his chair almost fell over.

"So what happens?" he asked, raking a hand through already-disheveled hair.

"We'll know more after the biopsy and surgery," the doctor said to Christoph. Then he turned to me again. "I don't want to scare you. The diagnosis is not easy. Unfortunately, we have to assume the liver tumor is a metastasis—that the cancer has already spread." He looked at me. Was he waiting for a response? A reaction?

I couldn't think of anything to say. I just couldn't seem to process this information. It was all so unreal. Why should this happen to me? I didn't feel all *that* sick. I only had a fever and sometimes stomachaches. I was healthy!

Christoph was beside himself; he paced the small room. And me? I felt calm, relaxed. Or maybe just empty . . . I simply didn't understand what I'd just heard.

Chapter 7
Mia—No More Long-term Goals

En route to Budapest, June 2012

An hour had passed since I'd boarded the train. An hour in which I'd tried to tune out the world around me. I'd kicked off my brown cowboy boots, put up my feet on the seat in front of me, and watched the world fly by outside the window. Green fields, mountains, highways. Loud music through the earbuds I wore guaranteed not a single other sound could penetrate.

But loud music couldn't drown out the voices in my head. I tried to concentrate on breathing evenly and closed my eyes. I felt the rhythm of my heart. I tried to focus on nothing except myself. Myself.

Without success.

My thoughts kept wandering back to the days I so wanted to banish from my memory.

. . .

Once I had finally processed the diagnosis—malignant melanoma—my entire world had shattered. I was deprived of everything that had been dear to me. I was tied to the bed and could no longer go to work.

During the first several days, I had no idea what "having cancer" meant. I wavered between courage over my diagnosis and ignorance of the scope of my disease. My body didn't feel much different. But an uneasy sensation became my steady companion. I knew something existed inside that was not meant to.

After surgery, everything was different. It was *real*. I had cancer. Recovery and continuing treatment made me dizzy and exhausted; I slept for days at a time. It dawned on me I'd be spending the foreseeable future in this bleak hospital room with naked walls. My mother offered to stay overnight with me, but I refused. I wanted her to lead her own life, the one she was used to.

Of course she couldn't do it. Nobody could. My family, my friends—everybody was suffering in their own way, but nobody wanted to admit it. I noticed, though. Everybody acted strangely, trying to cling to what was now gone. There was a lot of false cheer and overly bright jabbering, and always that one question: "How are you feeling?"

My family wanted to be constantly with me. I didn't want them there. I wanted them to lead their lives outside the hospital. Only I and my life needed to be confined.

Yet despite my appeals, they found it difficult to leave me by myself. The uncertainty of what was happening was hard on them. It was as if they thought their presence could create a favorable outcome.

Once I regained some strength, I was released and allowed to go home. Home, to my parents' house. It was my mother's idea that I move in with them. She thought she'd worry less with me there. I was so disheartened and weak, I agreed without giving it much thought. I abandoned my first apartment just like that. Even though my apartment was small, I'd made it cozy, thoughtfully decorating it with inexpensive furniture from IKEA, drawings I'd created, and photographs of my friends on the walls. Most of all, though, it had been mine. But just like that, I abandoned it.

As it turned out, my mother's idea had been wise. I was very grateful for her support, especially her emotional support. Christoph was very detached in those first weeks of my illness, when I'd needed him the most. The next steps of my recovery, though, sounded equally daunting.

The doctors explained the chemo and interferon-alpha therapies, which would begin once my body had recovered from surgery and my circulatory system was sufficiently stabilized.

The dermatologist, Dr. Oberbichler, also informed me about the side effects, both negative and positive. I had no clue what he could possibly mean by *positive* side effects. Everything I heard was negative: nausea, vomiting, fatigue, brittle nails, weakened sense of taste, loss of hair.

His words scared me.

As time grew near for my discharge, he added, "From now on, every new day is a day you need to win. Day after day. This is not about long-term goals anymore."

I was stunned. *No more long-term goals.*

Things didn't look hopeful: not for me, not for my body. All those negative side effects Dr. Oberbichler had warned me about happened, and then those words: *Why me?* They'd been a severe blow. I believed I had been well prepared for what to expect, but I'd been wrong.

Lounging on the train, I told myself it was the time to wind up the past, to look ahead, but I kept replaying events from the past year, kept hearing his words. Everything was etched on my mind. I had to find a way erase it all and start over. Wasn't this trip supposed to lead me to my new life?

Chapter 7 ½
Mia—Yet Another Thursday

Graz, April 2012

It was yet another Thursday. I hated Thursdays. I had to visit Dr. Weiß on Thursdays. Sometimes I talked. Most times I didn't, and we would sit in silence for an hour and a half. The only sounds were the ticking of a pendulum clock or the rustling pages in Dr. Weiß's notebook. Or the creaking of his leather chair whenever he shifted his position. Or the scribbling of his pen. Occasionally, he would take off his shoes and walk back and forth on the light gray shag carpet, hands clasped behind his back.

He tried to respect my space. He knew what made me tick and when it was OK to speak. I admit I wasn't an easy patient. The first three times he'd tried to engage me had been disastrous. The first time, I simply refused to speak. The second time, I threw a tantrum and smashed the red ceramic vase sitting on his coffee table. The third time, I grabbed my bag and ran out the door. Since then, he left me in peace unless I signaled my willingness to talk.

During those ninety minutes, I didn't move. When I did decide to talk, I rambled, speaking off the top of my head. With my mind on constant alert, as if danger lay around every corner, I was not sure I made any sense. My mind never rested. Neither did I.

Dr. Weiß was not my first therapist, but he was the only one who hadn't given up on me. Initially, after my suicide attempt, I'd refused to speak to any professional. I still didn't like therapy, but I'd eventually found some sort of comfort in my regular visits with Dr. Weiß. He was tactful; he simply let me be myself. And if that meant remaining quiet, we were quiet. He challenged me only when he felt I was strong enough for confrontation.

"How are you feeling today, Mia?" He always started us off with the same question. He leaned forward, his elbows on his knees.

I inhaled deeply, glanced at the stucco ceiling, and exhaled slowly. I shifted, making myself comfortable on the red leather Bordeaux sofa.

As always, Dr. Weiß waited patiently for my answer. My usual answer. I think I always said the same thing in the belief that if I just repeated it often enough, it'd be true. Without any inflection in my voice I said, "I'm feeling fine, Dr. Weiß. Just terrific."

He sighed loudly, leaned back, and crossed his legs. "Sometimes you act like a stubborn toddler, Mia," he said in his calm, sonorous voice. "You're twenty-four years old."

I jumped in before he could launch into a lecture. "Maybe that's exactly what I want to be. A toddler. Maybe I'm, like, tired of being twenty-four years old."

That might actually be the truth.

"I hear you. So let's skip the preliminaries."

I nodded.

"I would like to discuss something with you today. We've been making slow progress, and while I do see improvements, it will still be a long and difficult journey before you're able to feel joy again. I hope you'll get there sooner rather than later, but I'm confident you *will* get there, eventually."

I looked away, avoiding his glance. He was really good. Without ever having talked about it, he knew exactly what I longed for so desperately.

"I just think we got stuck here a little bit . . ."

I jerked my head up and stared at him, terrified. He wanted to get rid of me, just like the others. Despair swept over me. Dr. Weiß was the first therapist who'd tried to understand me.

"Don't worry," he said softly. "Listen to me. I am not ending our collaboration. That wouldn't be productive."

I felt a big lump in my throat and swallowed hard. I wanted to continue our sessions. Even if I didn't act like it.

"This place, this city is significantly hindering your emotional recovery. There are too many memories. Memories you want to escape."

I listened to him intently.

"You should consider going on a trip. You are well, overall. You are no longer suicidal. You just need to learn to let go. I know you'll hate me for bringing this up again, but I strongly advise you to start journaling. You need to let the past be the past. You are still alive."

Alive. Well. *Still* . . .

Dr. Weiß stood, walked around his desk, and sat next to me on the sofa. "Mia, you've already won the major battle. Your body has fought back as best as it could. Now you need to learn how to experience joy in what you have, even if it doesn't look the way you'd like it to." He continued, "I'll respect your decision, whatever it will be. I am not trying to persuade you. I am trying only to make things easier for you."

I turned to face Dr. Weiß. My nervous habit returned—I began to chew on my lower lip. I was grateful to Dr. Weiß for his understanding and for always pushing me in the right direction. If I really wanted joy again, I would have to learn to loosen up and, as he put it, let go.

"You need to leave for a while," he said quietly. "Go on a trip. Away from this town. Stay wherever you go as long as you need, until you feel joy again. Put your pain on paper, and when there is nothing left to say, burn the journal. Relearn how to live; let the past stay in the past. Begin a new life."

Chapter 8
Mia—Everything Is OK

En route to Budapest, June 2012

I grabbed my journal and a pen, ready to put my thoughts on paper. Maybe it would help, after all.

But before I could begin, my glance fell on my old sketchbook and new monolith pencils tucked into a side pocket on my backpack. My mother must have put them there. It'd been a long time since I'd done any drawing. With trembling hands, I reached for the sketchbook and slowly leafed through it.

I looked at every drawing. Dr. Weiß had encouraged me to do things I loved. He said they'd help me feel like myself again.

Just looking at the sketches wouldn't teach me how to feel joy again, but understanding how I had seen the world might be useful. They conveyed the happiness I'd once felt and wanted to feel again, even if only briefly. As if remotely controlled, my fingers grabbed up a pencil, and I began to draw.

The implement flew across the paper. I didn't think about what I was depicting until I'd finished.

Then I contemplated the result for a long time. Out of the palm of a hand grew a shoot. In one corner of the paper, I had written "New Beginning." Yes, that was it. Now. Here. A new beginning.

I held on tight to the sketchbook and closed my eyes. Something inside me felt lighter. What was most strange, though, was I even felt a timid smile on my face.

I started awake with a bad cramp in my right hand.

"Damn it!" I yelled and jumped to my feet. The meds had destroyed my magnesium balance and often caused horrible spasms. If I forgot to take a single pill to prevent it, my body punished me. My stiff fingers bent at odd angles, out of my control. The worst cramping often hit me whenever I'd gripped something tightly or at night as I slept. And this was one of the worst.

I frantically shook my arm and massaged the muscles, cursing under my breath.

"Is everything OK?"

Startled, I looked to my left. A young man was sitting across the aisle. Even seated, I could tell he was tall and well built.

He gazed at me with caring big gray eyes. I couldn't look away. Somehow, I'd become entangled in his glance, even though I was still desperately trying to get rid of the spasm.

"Is everything OK?" he asked again. His deep voice brought me back to the here and now. I must have been gawking, but I found it difficult to turn away from those eyes.

"Um . . . yes," I stammered. "It'll be all right in a minute." Summoning every bit of strength, I tried to escape the magnetism of his gaze. But it was as if I were hypnotized, unable to look away. Those eyes . . . they were mesmerizing. So dark, you could barely separate pupils from irises. They were all deep gray shimmer.

I kept staring—until I finally realized who he was.

Without saying another word, I turned away brusquely and sat down again.

Chapter 9
Samuel—A New Beginning

Vienna, June 2012

I rushed up the stairs to the platform. The escalator was far too slow, and waiting for an elevator was out of the question. A heavy knapsack hung from my back, but I managed to jump on board the train before the doors closed. I would have been at the station earlier had I not stayed out so late the night before. I hadn't slept because when I'd returned home, I'd remembered I hadn't yet packed my stuff.

My friends had insisted on painting the town one last time. How could I refuse? There was always a good reason to celebrate with them. This time it was to bid me farewell before I departed on my new life.

The train picked up speed while I was still leaning against the wall, trying to catch my breath after the frantic sprint through the station. Eventually, my heart rate slowed. I ran a hand through my hair, inhaled deeply, and walked down the aisle. Fortunately, the train was rather empty, and there were many free rows. In one of the seats, I noticed a young woman.

I put my baggage down and sat across the aisle from her.

I eyed her curiously. She was sleeping, and a slight smile played around her lips. Judging from her expression, she was at peace with the world.

I studied her intently and observed the steady rising and falling of her chest. She was clasping a small black sketchbook with her thin fingers. They seemed almost too thin. The nails had been bitten to the quick; I could see they had been bleeding.

I realized if anyone saw me staring the way I was, I'd seem like a stalker.

But I wasn't. I'd simply never seen a woman so fascinating that I'd wanted to study her like this. Something about this woman captivated me.

She appeared to be quite skinny, or maybe she just seemed so because her lilac blouse hung loosely on her frame. The top had long sleeves, in contrast to her gray shorts, which were quite short. Short strands of blond hair peeked out from under the gray knitted hat she wore. I couldn't imagine why she wore a hat, given that it was June. But it looked great on her.

Her face was magnificently beautiful, with a sweet button nose and soft pink lips. But her looks weren't everything. She emanated something very special. It was impossible to look away.

"Damn it!" she suddenly screeched. Had I not already been staring at her, I would have done so now. Other passengers twisted their necks to see what was happening, only to shrug and turn back to their conversations, books, or other activities.

Yep, that was what our society had become. Nobody cared. Everyone lived in their own bubbles, only for themselves. Had someone been shot, the reactions wouldn't have been much different.

Maybe I shouldn't have judged. I was just as egotistical as the next person. But not on this day. My curiosity about this woman made me more empathetic.

She frantically jerked about, shaking her right hand. I watched for a while. She didn't even notice my newborn-stalker-self, because her eyes were still shut. Her entire body was tense, and her face contorted with pain. I could see little wrinkles crease her forehead.

"Is everything OK?" I asked.

She stopped moving and opened her eyes wide. Those eyes . . . They were vast and green. No, not green . . . emerald. Never before had I seen eyes like hers. I had already thought this woman was attractive. I had even more evidence now.

She didn't answer, she only stared at me. She was still holding her right hand, massaging it. But her body had visibly relaxed. The wrinkles on her forehead disappeared and her shoulders dropped. A healthy pink now colored her cheeks. She looked perfect. I was hypnotized.

I rubbed my face, then my eyes, and shook my head, trying to regain control of my thoughts.

"Is everything OK?" I repeated gently.

For a brief moment, she closed her eyes and breathed deeply. Then there they were again . . . those huge emerald eyes. She exhaled.

She opened her mouth, blinked a few times, then closed it again. There was a moment of silence before she cleared her throat and softly said, "Um . . . Yes. It'll be all right in a minute."

Her voice was . . . wow. Enchanting. Bright and clear. But I could hear an underlying sadness. Although she tried to appear cheerful, that poignant tone gave her away.

I smiled at her, hoping for a smile in return. But she just widened her eyes and stared at me, as if suddenly terrified, then quickly turned away.

I was startled by her behavior, but why shouldn't she react like that? I was a stranger, and she didn't know what I might want from her. Why was I gawking at her like that, anyway?

All I wanted was to sit here peacefully and enjoy my alone time. But the events that had caused me to abandon my former life replayed in my mind.

Chapter 9 ½
Samuel—I'm Not Doing This

Vienna, May 2012

"Hey there, buddy." Without knocking first, my dad, CEO of the architectural firm I worked for, entered my office. He approached behind me, then put one hand on my shoulder. Quickly, I finished typing an e-mail, hit "Send," and turned around. I crossed my legs and leaned back in my chair.

"What can I do for you?" I asked.

"Just wanted to bring you some documents," my father said and handed me a thick binder.

I looked at him and raised my eyebrows. "That's what you come to my office for? Is your secretary on vacation?"

Matthias Winter laughed his deep, sonorous laugh. "No, no. These are important, and I wanted to personally ensure you got them."

I shook my head. "Right, because Brigitte would have lost them," I said, giving him a look. My father would have been adrift without her. She organized everything—private and professional meetings, all his correspondence. Sometimes I wondered whether she also cooked for him and did his laundry. Brigitte was more than a secretary. She was his veritable girl Friday. She would never lose any documents.

"Well, this binder was supposed to get to you earlier. But that's not important now. What is important is I'm giving you your own project."

I jumped from my chair with such enthusiasm that it almost toppled over.

"Really?" I asked. I had been working in my father's architecture firm as junior officer for six months, but so far, he hadn't let me oversee any projects. All I did was administrative work, the same as I had been doing for him since I was in college. I was nothing more than a second secretary.

"Take it easy, son. Familiarize yourself with these papers, then come to my office so we can discuss the details," he said.

"Yessss!" I pumped a fist in the air after he'd closed the door behind him. I had been working toward this moment. Finally, I had a chance to prove myself.

I opened the binder and studied every page, then leafed through it again, more quickly. I hesitated and scrutinized the notes again. He couldn't be serious. Was this a test?

I snapped the binder shut and paced my office. With one hand I massaged my neck, and with the other, I ran my fingers through my hair, muttering quietly, "He can't be doing this. Is this the first time? Or have I signed off on this garbage before? I don't look at everything in detail. Damn it." I punched my right fist against the wall. Pain radiated up my arm. Shit. Too hard.

I grabbed the notebook and stomped out of the office. I slammed my door and stormed my father's antechamber.

Brigitte, who was sitting behind her computer, let out a scream. "Oh my god, Mr. Winter, you scared me." I apologized and, still in a fury, wrenched open my father's office door, leaving Brigitte in my wake. "Mr. Winter. Mr. Winter!"

I didn't bother turning around.

"Samuel, you can't go in there now!"

I raised my hand, motioning for her to stop. She clammed up immediately. The only sound was the clicking of her heels on the old parquet as she retreated.

Grim-faced, I stood in the doorway. I was breathing heavily, shaking. I was livid, unbelievably livid. Why had he never said a word? I was angry with myself for having been so blind to what was really going on.

"Samuel, we're in a meeting," my father snapped.

I ignored his remark and entered the room. His executive board members watched me under lowered brows, but I didn't care. I wanted everyone to know how my father was running his business.

He rose from his pretentious-looking black leather chair, straightened his tie, and buttoned his jacket. "Samuel!" he barked again in a deep voice.

I tossed the binder onto the table. His expression turned puzzled. I glared at him while he picked it up.

"What—?"

"No, not *what*," I hissed. "*How. How* often? *How* many times have you done this?"

"Not here, Samuel. Let's discuss this later," he said, his voice calm. Judging from his demeanor, he felt no guilt; he had done this many times. Taken homes from people. How could I not have known?

"You feel good about yourself? How can you sleep at night?" I snapped.

My father grabbed my arm and ushered me to the door. Before we exited, he turned to his board members. "Gentlemen, please excuse us for a moment. I'll have Brigitte serve you some refreshments, and if you like, go to lunch without me."

The five men nodded.

Once out of their sight, my father practically dragged me through the antechamber, then opened the door and shoved me into the corridor.

"What was that all about? What were you thinking?" he growled.

I smiled bitterly and shook my head. "What was *I* thinking? What are *you* thinking? Had I known the games you're playing, I would have never joined this company."

"Ah, so that's what this is about." He stood there, motionless, not blinking an eye. How cold he was.

"You can live with this? You're the reason for hundreds of people losing their homes, damn it. People who can't afford to go anywhere else!"

My father crossed his arms and listened as I continued to yell. Once I'd sputtered to a halt, he said, "My son, that's business. *Our* business. Old buildings get demolished; new ones get built. Those still living in the old buildings have to move. They're mostly tenements, no longer profitable and already half-empty. Only old people remain, because who wants to live there? We give other people what they want. Shopping malls, bank branches—you name it. We breathe new life into dead neighborhoods all over the world. *It's called business.*"

"Yeah, that's what you call it. You could renovate those buildings, make them desirable again. New families could move in. That's another way to *breathe new life* into a neighborhood. Without evicting anybody," I spat.

"That's not how things work, son." he said.

I could only shake my head. I fisted my hands in my hair, unable to fathom his callous, cruel practices. That's how he'd had made it to the top? That's how he could afford jetting around the world? By depriving the poor and catering to the rich?

I inhaled deeply and massaged my temples, shifting my weight from one leg to the other. "Now I understand why everyone hates you," I said. No answer. No reaction. *Nothing.*

I dropped my hands, crossed my arms. We stared at each other for a long time, our stances identical. I saw my father's matching anger in the tension in his jaw and the pulsating veins in his throat.

Did I want what he had? Could I stomach what he did? I wanted to be an architect but not at any cost. Not here. Not where the price was human dignity.

I yanked my black tie from around my neck and threw it at his feet. "I'm out of here. You can go on without me. I'm not doing this. Find another model for your ads. It makes me sick to think people will identify my face with your dirty practices."

His expression turned even grimmer. He took a step toward me until our faces were only inches apart. He hissed through his teeth. "What do you think I trained you for all those years? Why did I encourage you to finish school early? Why did I pay for all that education, for all that you have, when you're letting me down now? A true son doesn't behave like this. A true son works side by side with his father in the family business and supports his decisions. I've built this company so that you could own it one day, lead a good life like me. And now you're throwing it all away? That's foolishness!"

"No, Dad, it's not. Find another face. Find another idiot, one who doesn't care what you do. Leave *him* all your money. I'm out of here." I turned my back and walked away.

I heard him holler behind me, "Don't count on any further support. From now on, you're on your own!" And then I heard my father say, "You're no longer my son."

I froze, trying to understand what that would mean to me. To be on my own. Then I moved on, into a new life.

Chapter 10
Samuel—Am I a Stalker?

En route to Budapest, June 2012

I rose from my seat and stepped into the aisle, where her black sketchbook was still lying on the floor. She apparently hadn't noticed it had fallen.

I picked it up to hand it to her. She'd closed her eyes again, her chest gently rising and falling. She'd tucked up her legs, and her arms were wrapped around her knees. Her entire appearance was different now.

When I'd first seen her sleeping, she'd seemed happy and at peace, but now . . . Now she seemed fragile, vulnerable . . . as if she needed protection to keep the world at bay.

She was so still. How could someone fall asleep so fast? It hadn't been more than five minutes since she'd settled down.

I was still holding her book. Looking down, I opened to the page marked by a ribbon. I couldn't help myself. It seemed important that I know more about her.

I saw an astonishingly skilled pencil drawing showing the vigorous new growth of a plant rooted in the palm of a hand. The rendering was amazing, the hand incredibly realistic. I was impressed.

My curiosity grew as I turned the pages. Countless drawings, each one better than the next—flowers, meadows, sunsets in a city. Life in all its vibrancy. Faces, laughter. Portraits of men and women, all depicted in high spirits. Many of the drawings were of one man, her artist's perspective capturing every angle of his face. His eyes. His mouth. He must be special to her.

On the last page, I found a self-portrait. The most beautiful smile I had ever seen on her face. Yet there was more to it. Her eyes beamed with the joy of being alive. With energy. Her loveliness was breathtaking. She looked the same right now on the train—and yet different.

In the drawing, an abundance of long, straight hair framed her face. As far as I could tell, she now had short hair under her hat.

"Give that to me!"

I started. She snatched the book out of my hands. Our fingertips touched, but only for a second.

I raised both hands, palms out, and apologized, "I'm sorry. I didn't mean to be rude. I only went to pick it up, but then . . ." I tried an apologetic smile and added, "You draw damn well."

She looked at me as if she wanted to kill me, pressing the sketchbook to her chest as if her life depended on it. Her breath had quickened. Her posture was stiff and her eyes wide, but her pupils were only pinpoints. I hoped she wasn't having a panic attack. Had I really infringed on her privacy that much?

I felt like a big asshole for leafing through the book without her permission. Usually I didn't do things like that. I mean, I would have been outraged, too, if someone didn't respect my privacy. But I simply couldn't stop myself. Once I'd started turning the pages, each sketch had pulled me onto the next. Her drawings were awesome. It was as if the deep emotions I sensed behind them were speaking to me. It was as if I were right there in them. With her.

When she didn't respond, I returned to my seat, but I couldn't seem to quit staring. It was as if it were impossible not to. What an idiot—I was coming across as a clueless jerk. Maybe even a stalker.

She was staring out the window. But I could tell by the tense way she held herself that she was aware of my gaze. And I must have stirred her curiosity, as well. I caught her throwing furtive, timid glances at me. Sometimes, when our glances met, I smiled, but she didn't smile back. Her emerald eyes just lingered a little longer each time, and I thought I detected a spark of interest, which encouraged me to keep my gaze pointed in her direction.

"I'm really sorry about what happened," I finally said. "It was rude to open your book. I usually wouldn't act like that, honest, but your drawings fascinated me."

Frowning at my words, she blinked, then shook her head and stared out the window again. But she kept casting those glances over at me.

I should leave her alone. But there was something about her . . . I wanted her to look at me again. Then keep looking at me. I needed to see her eyes. I needed to hear her voice.

"I'm Samuel, by the way . . . Sam," I said, breaking the silence.

Her gaze flickered, then she loosened the tight grip around the book and eventually placed it on the small table in front of her.

My instincts continued to tell me to leave her alone. But I couldn't. I looked from her to her luggage, a big backpack. She was traveling on a Eurail pass, most likely. But why would a woman like her journey alone?

Suddenly, she froze, her body tensing again. She fisted her hands so tight that her knuckles turned white. Droplets of blood appeared on her palms as her nails pressed deeply into her skin. It was almost too much to watch. Why did she inflict so much pain on herself? I scrambled for some way to distract her from whatever thoughts had led to her reaction.

"Are you going to Budapest? Or are you connecting there?" I realized my intentions went beyond distracting her. I also just wanted to know. I suspected my friendliness, though, was probably only frightening her. Why wouldn't she speak with me?

As I had before, I heard her inhale, then exhale. Like one of those relaxation techniques, maybe to control her nervousness. Then she finally looked into my eyes, without saying a word.

And I drowned in an emerald sea.

She needed no words to communicate; she spoke with her eyes. She was tired. Not tired in the sense of wanting to sleep. It was something different. Exhaustion. Sluggishness. Something she was missing.

She held my gaze, blinking only occasionally, still doing those rhythmic breaths. Eventually, I noted her muscles relax. Her fists loosened, and she wiped the blood on her palms off on her dark gray jean shorts. She didn't seem to care if they got stained. Or maybe she didn't notice. She continued staring and waited through a few more breaths before finally speaking.

"So, you like to sneak through other people's stuff?" She sounded annoyed.

It wasn't what I had hoped for, but she had a point.

I scratched the back of my head. "Look, as I said, I'm really sorry. Your book was on the floor in the aisle. I didn't want anybody to step on it. I wanted to give it to you. Then I looked at that drawing. I was fascinated and began to leaf through it." I looked at her apologetically. "It won't happen again."

She blinked again and whispered, "OK." That was all.

Chapter 10 ½
Mia—Nothing Is OK

Graz, December 2011

No, I was not OK. Nothing was OK. Everything sucked. Everything made me want to throw up. And throw up I did, constantly.

I wanted to pull my hair, which I would have, had there been any left to pull. I wanted to scream so loudly that the whole world shattered.

Anxiously, I looked around the room. I scratched the scar on my arm. The pain reminded me that I was still here.

I heard the soothing voice of Dr. Weiß. "I'm here, Mia. And so are you. Everything is OK." I stared into his eyes, without focusing. "Breathe evenly, like we practiced."

I looked to the side. With the exception of my fingers still scratching where I'd cut myself, I didn't move. I couldn't do what he wanted. My head felt as if it would explode any minute. I sensed an oncoming panic attack. I was panting. My body had stiffened. I couldn't control the spasms in my muscles, which just about knocked me out. So much for *everything is OK*.

I'm not well. How can anyone deal with a situation like this? No, no, I'm not well. Nothing is OK.

I will *be OK, though. Just not today or even tomorrow. One day, though . . . Maybe.*

"Mia, listen to me." I stared at my therapist. "Relax your hands. Leave the scars alone. Breathe calmly. Inhale and exhale." He raised his arms to signal when I needed to inhale, and lowered them when he wanted me to exhale. My heart rate slowed. I stopped scratching. Dr. Weiß motioned for me to flex my fingers.

"Just do as I do. Don't forget to breathe."

I took in mouthfuls of air, normally and slowly. The feeling I was going to explode any minute finally vanished.

He smiled. "You're doing great."

I smiled wearily. *Doing great.* I shouldn't be needing to do this at all.

"What happened? Where were you?"

My expression darkened immediately. I didn't want to remember the trigger for my reactions. It would propel me back to my previous state. I wasn't ready to discuss what set me off. I needed to know how to prevent the spasms, that's all. I squirmed, nervously tapping my foot and worrying my lower lip.

"Mia," I heard Dr. Weiß's voice. "Breathe. You can do it. Tell me what led you to panic. Breathe evenly. You can do it," he said again.

I can do it.

Hoarsely, I said, "I—I—"

"Keep breathing," my therapist repeated.

"It's the . . . the question." I inhaled and exhaled and paused. I needed to maintain my control. Otherwise, I would suffer another attack. Dr. Weiß sat in his leather chair and waited.

"It's the *OK*, the saying *OK*," I said quickly. Done. It was out, and I was still there. No panic attack.

"Very good, Mia. I knew you could do it." He leaned forward, his elbows propped on his knees. "And now I'd like to know why that's the case."

"Why . . . ?" I squeezed all the air from my lungs. "How often can you hear a phrase before you feel you need to puke? Can you stand to hear it every day? Several times a day? I can't," I said quietly.

He looked at me and frowned. "How do you mean?"

"Nothing is OK. *OK?*" My voice grew louder. "Every day, I hear everything's OK, everything's fine. *Nothing* is fine. Nothing will ever be fine. For god's sake, don't you ever look at me? Look at me! What's OK about me? Skinny, hollow cheeks, almost no hair. My body is a shell," I yelled at him, then added, barely audible, "an empty shell."

He nodded. "You are a strong person. Believe me when I tell you that you will heal and that you will live. Everything *will* be OK." He rose, moved over to me, and patted my shoulder. "Remember how far you've come. You're alive. You've survived the worst. You're making progress here." He smiled at me.

I had no clue how to answer and just stared at him blankly.

"Appreciate what you've already achieved, Mia. Focus on that, not on how far you still have to go. I know you're not where you want to be, but you're also not where you were anymore."

I responded with a faint smile.

I was not OK. But I would be. Not today, not tomorrow . . . *someday*.

Chapter 11
Mia—Soothing Eyes

En route to Budapest, June 2012

Everything was OK.

The guy was only giving me back my sketchbook. Or was intending to give it back, before he'd started poking around inside. I hated when people looked at my drawings without permission. My sketchbook was private.

Then, when he did hand it to me, our fingertips touched. It was only a very brief, light touch, but my body immediately went into defense mode. Anxiety gripped me. I sensed an emerging panic attack. I breathed evenly, stretching my hands, clenching and unclenching my fingers. Dr. Weiß's damned breathing technique wasn't helping much, though. It always took too long to relax me. And those pointed glances that guy was throwing my way weren't helping any.

I had barely begun my trip, and someone was already on my case. No, not just someone—Samuel Winter, the bulldozer, demolisher of human lives. I'd seen the newspaper ads sporting his image plenty of times, so I'd recognized him right off. If you dug even a little into the architecture and real-estate world, it didn't take long to understand what kind of business he was in. Nobody wrote much about it. Things like that got covered up. But my coworkers and I had stumbled onto the truth. How could he lend his face to something so underhanded?

I ignored him. I didn't feel like small talk, and certainly no small talk with him. Though I would have loved to look into those eyes once more.

So I finally turned around.

Incredibly long eyelashes framed his dark gray eyes. He was smiling broadly. I knew about his company's dirty schemes and would never want to socialize with someone like him, but I couldn't help being intrigued. He was stunning. More good-looking than any newspaper ad could convey. Far too good-looking. He was tall. Taller than I had first thought. Wavy black hair. The light stubble on his jaw and slightly crooked nose completed his perfect appearance. He was manly. Sexy.

He continued to smile at me without saying a word. At first, I was speechless, hooked by those shimmering eyes. Somehow, they soothed me. The beat of my heart calmed. My body relaxed. I was less fearful of speaking.

"So, you like to sneak through other people's stuff?" I'd sounded harsher than I'd intended.

I turned my back on him again and tried hard to ignore him. It would have been far easier had he not been sitting across from me. I didn't feel like company, even his company–especially his company. I was already overwhelmed by my own.

I must have dozed off. When someone gently shook my shoulder, I sprang awake in alarm. Frozen, breath caught in my throat, I hoped whoever it was would just go away.

Thank you . . . now leave. I gasped for some air and tried to suppress my rising fear, biting my lower lip until I tasted blood.

Finally, I opened my eyes, blinking rapidly until they adjusted to the harsh overhead light. Outside it was dark. I could see the orange lights of a station's platform illuminating the scenery—people racing to catch trains, people waiting, people laughing and busy with normal lives, full of energy.

"We've arrived in Budapest. You need to get off," Samuel said and gestured toward the exit. He had on his backpack and was holding a guitar.

Unhurriedly, I stood up and stretched, slung on my backpack, then headed toward the door, Samuel a few steps behind me. At the exit, I paused, took a deep breath, and turned around.

"Thank you for waking me up." My voice was calmer now. He meant well. He had given me my sketchbook and woke me up, and, unlike all the uncaring people who'd simply stared when I'd yelped in pain when my muscles had cramped, he had asked whether everything was all right.

I faked a smile, then hopped off the train, and started to hurry away.

"You're welcome," he called.

Abruptly, I stopped and looked back at him. "I'm sorry for being so rude. I . . ." I dropped my gaze. "I guess I just don't like anyone seeing my drawings."

"No worries." He moved up alongside me. "I deserved it. I wouldn't want anyone to sneak through my private stuff. I just couldn't resist." I could see the honesty in his eyes. I had never met anyone whose eyes revealed so much. They had a magic appeal.

A smile toyed on his lips. I was shamelessly checking him out, but I wasn't embarrassed. I felt no hint of an oncoming panic attack. As long as I looked into those soothing eyes, I felt strangely sheltered.

"Let's just start from the beginning," he said with a wink. "I'm Samuel Winter. You can call me Sam." He extended his hand and waited for mine.

Winter... Did I want to know a Winter?

Before he could touch my hand, I hid it behind my back. He frowned and looked puzzled. I didn't—couldn't—manage handshakes anymore. I tried to feign another smile, hoping it would dispel the sudden awkwardness, but I've always been bad at faking things. Awkwardness, though, was far better than having to touch or be touched. Anything was.

"I'm Mia Lang," I blurted, sure I came across as a total nutcase.

Sam lowered his hand to his side. "Pleased to meet you, Mia Lang. Where are you headed?"

Out of here as fast as possible. Since saying my thought out loud seemed a poor option, I answered, "Bed. And then . . . we'll see." He grinned. I continued, "Hope you have a great trip. Good night."

I left before he could say anything else.

Chapter 12
Mia—Let Me Sleep

Budapest, June 2012

I made my way toward the station's exit. I had deliberately chosen Budapest as my first stop. The city was familiar and held warm memories, although it seemed an eternity had passed since I'd last been here.

I had spent half a semester here during college. Many of my classmates had chosen to go to an English-speaking country, but I'd wanted to stay close to my family. And close to Christoph.

While it wasn't just a hop between Graz and Budapest, it was not as far away as the UK or somewhere overseas.

Spending time in Hungary had turned out to be the right decision. I'd had many experiences that'd proved valuable, both for my career and for life in general. I'd been on my own for the first time and learned to fend for myself.

I'd loved the city, and it hadn't taken long to find new companions. I hadn't always been the recluse I was now.

On my first day there, I'd met Kriszta, who would become one of my best friends. She'd worked in the cafe below the tiny apartment I'd rented for four months.

That day, I'd planned to grab a coffee, then explore the neighborhood, but I'd not left the place until after closing because the two of us had instantly hit it off.

We'd been strangers, but it sure hadn't felt that way. She'd been so easy to talk with; her German was excellent, which had helped. We'd hung out almost daily after that, but sadly, we'd lost touch after I'd returned home.

I wondered whether she still worked in the cafe and decided to swing by after I settled in.

I hailed a cab and gave the driver the address of the hotel I'd booked. I couldn't afford much, although I was craving the comfort of a nice place. That craving intensified when I entered the hotel room and saw the bed. Maybe I should shell out more the next time, I thought.

I was so tired I decided I didn't care. All I wanted was to lie down and shut my eyes, although I'd slept for hours on the train.

I tossed the backpack in a corner and threw myself onto the squeaking, metal-framed bed. The yellowing sheets, which may have been white at some point in the past, were itchy and stiff. I felt every single spring in the mattress but couldn't be bothered to lodge a protest. I was exhausted. I wanted only to sleep—and not dream of anything unsettling.

Unfortunately, Samuel's dark gaze haunted me, and tired as I was, I still had trouble drifting off. Why couldn't I let go of his image? Why couldn't I just forget his eyes? They seemed so familiar, as if they saw straight into me and knew my deepest secrets. My biggest fears. On the train, anxiety had nearly overwhelmed me as usual, but when I'd looked into his eyes, I'd grown entirely relaxed.

Why him? He had seemed so nice and kind, so different from the rumors that followed him. Maybe I shouldn't have been so judgmental.

Maybe I should have changed my attitude for the sake of making a new connection. But my inner self had screamed, demanding I leave the stranger alone. Everyone was barred from entering my world.

I lay awake thinking about Samuel for a long time before a restless sleep finally descended.

Chapter 13
Samuel—Many Mistakes

Budapest, June 2012

Damn it . . . Why had I let her slip away? Why hadn't I managed to really talk to her? Back on the train, I'd been so bemused when she finally did speak to me, I'd hardly made sense, so no wonder she'd likely not even registered a word of what I'd said, even though I'd been right across the aisle.

I'd waited for a reaction from her, but there'd been only a few harsh words. Then she'd slept like the dead, legs tucked up. Only when I'd examined her carefully could I see she was still breathing.

I worked to stop staring, as I had for the entire trip. Some ancestor definitely had passed down stalker genes to me. Looking for distraction, I grabbed my guitar, leaned back, and played some random melodies, stopping every now and then to scribble notes on a piece of paper. And finally, the train reached Budapest.

Budapest was one of the few major cities in Europe I'd never visited, so I thought it an ideal starting point for my travels.

I grabbed my things, then my glance fell on her again. She was still sleeping. I didn't want to leave her there, so vulnerable and alone. Likely nobody else would bother to wake her, except maybe the conductor. I hesitated, then decided I couldn't let the opportunity to talk with her one last time pass.

Gently, I shook her shoulder until she opened her eyes. Dark had fallen. The light overhead glared into her eyes. She blinked, then she actually talked to me. I mean, she had to—how could she continue ignoring a guy who was stalking her, right? It seemed as if I had internalized some of my father's lectures on perseverance.

When we reached the exit, she turned, and in a voice sweet as honey, said, "Thank you for waking me up." She jumped down the steps and hurried off so fast, she was almost running. That didn't stop me from calling "You're welcome" after her.

Abruptly, she stopped and looked back at me. Looking sheepish, she said, "You know, I'm sorry for being so rude. I . . . I guess I just don't like anyone seeing my drawings."

She'd apologized for my behavior! She hadn't needed to.

I assured her I deserved every bit of her anger, then smiled at her. "Let's just start from the beginning. I'm Samuel Winter. You can call me Sam," I said and extended my hand. Quickly, she tucked hers behind her back, her face turning ashen. Her lips curved into an artificial smile. But she spoke. "I'm Mia Lang."

Mia. The name suited her perfectly. I still wore my smile, and I asked her whether she was staying in Budapest or continuing elsewhere. She turned and left without answering.

Not knowing what to make of her behavior, I felt even more curious than I had before. I decided I'd look her up online after I reached my hotel. Maybe I'd find some answers.

Outside the station, cabs waited in a long row. I told the driver to take me to whatever first-class hotel he'd recommend, that expense was not a problem. The only thing I wanted was the availability of breakfast in the morning. Since this had all been a last-minute decision, I'd done no planning. I simply wanted to disappear from my life for a while, a life that had been chained to an agenda for far too long. I'd arrived at my first stop, Budapest. Right now, that's all I needed to know.

The cab dropped me off at a place downtown. The room was spacious—unnecessarily spacious. After all, only I'd be sleeping here. The advantage of a good hotel, though, was that I could order room service anytime. I picked up the phone; I was starving.

After I'd eaten, I fell into bed like a stone. It was late, past eleven. I wanted to get up early and explore the city.

Yet I couldn't fall asleep, despite the comfortable bed with its soft mattress, huge pillow, and freshly scented duvet.

Too many thoughts raced through my head. Thoughts I wanted to avoid. Thoughts I couldn't erase. How could I have taken a job, loaned my face and my reputation to an enterprise, even my dad's, that was so underhanded? I hated myself for my decisions, the decisions that had compelled me to take this trip, and for not examining my father's methods more carefully. I swore never to do anything like that again. But I couldn't change the past. Still, realizing how ignorant, how selfish I'd been made me even angrier at myself. I tossed and turned. I hurled one of the pillows against the wall. Grabbed my hair. Felt a lump in my throat. I didn't want to think about the past any longer. Didn't want to shed any more tears. Had I answered the damned phone only once . . .

I would have known.

I should have known.

I needed to tune out my thoughts. I tried to chill out. But I couldn't. Not only did my thoughts trouble me, but every time I closed my eyes, I saw emerald green eyes. Their brilliance haunted me.

I had to find Mia again.

Chapter 14
Mia—Why Can't I Find Peace and Quiet?

Budapest, June 2012

The night was exhausting. I couldn't sleep. Usually, I was so dead to the world that I wouldn't wake if a bomb exploded next to my bed. But the motel-room bed was a joke. Plus, people were partying in the streets. Doors slammed in the corridor. Beds squeaked. My head throbbed like crazy. And my thoughts . . . Horrible thoughts of the past kept me awake. I hoped the next day would be better.

In the morning, I tugged a fresh shirt, my jean shorts, and my travel kit out of my backpack before I hurried into the bathroom. It was too hot for long pants. I was thankful the bathroom was adjacent to my room, so I could avoid other people staying on the same floor. I needed privacy. I didn't want anyone seeing my scars. Not the one on my right lower arm. Not the huge one on my stomach. Not the other smaller ones that pocked my body. The majority had healed into white ridges, but a few still shimmered with pink and reminded me of the most painful days. Whenever I was about to stumble off of the path toward a better life, I found myself scratching them. Maybe it was a nervous gesture, but it reminded me of where I never wanted to go again.

I stayed in the shower for a long time and let the warm water run down my body. It felt good, and I was able to relax. At least as long as I didn't have to touch my flesh. Washing my hair, or whatever you wanted to call the short feathers on my scalp, was still difficult.

After I got out of the shower I wrapped a peach-colored towel around my bony body. The sense of well-being I'd felt in the shower was already fading.

After dressing, I returned to my room and hastily stuffed all my belongings back into the backpack, then struggled with the zipper, wondering how they'd all possibly fit in there before. Once I'd gotten it closed, I shouldered the heavy thing and walked downstairs to the front desk.

"I'd like to check out please," I told the lady at the reception. She looked at me quizzically.

"Pay please," I tried again.

She just shook her head and raised her eyebrows.

Somewhere in a dark corner of my brain, I searched for what was left of my Hungarian.

"Fizetni kèrem," I stammered.

"Igen, igen," she smiled cheerfully and wrote the amount on a piece of paper.

I wandered the streets of Budapest. I knew the squares and tourist sites and didn't spend much time in any one place. Being here didn't make me happy, after all. Every corner brought back memories of better days, so many I wanted to cry. I started scratching at my scars again. My feet hurt. It was hot. I wanted to leave.

I rested for a while on a bench by a fountain in the city center near Váci Street, the famous pedestrian zone. Feeling exhausted, I leaned my head against the backpack and closed my eyes, hoping to find some peace. The sun shone on my face. It was a lovely June day. With my eyes still shut, I stretched out my legs and relaxed. The street wasn't very busy. Lost in my own world, I let the soft conversation and laughter around me mingle with my thoughts. I made up stories to match the voices, imagining the people they belonged to. I loved getting lost in those kinds of fantasies. They allowed me to disappear from this planet and slip into my own universe, where I could stop being myself.

I relaxed my arms and let my nails trail over the hard surface of the bench. Suddenly, my fingers encountered divots in the wood. Heart suddenly pounding, I opened my eyes, blinking until I'd again grown used to the sunshine.

Then I looked down. After all those years, the carving was still there. I caught my breath. I would not find peace and quiet today.

Chapter 14 ½
Mia—I Love You too, Christoph

Budapest, January 2009

My first week in Budapest was over. I enjoyed being away from home, yet I missed my parents, sister, and especially Christoph.

How was I supposed to live four months without him? We would see each other sporadically, but we couldn't afford to travel back and forth every weekend. We had to make this separation work somehow.

That Sunday in January, I'd planned to see my new friend, Kriszta, on her day off. She wanted to treat me to a private sightseeing tour, including the nightlife.

Half an hour before we were to meet, someone knocked on the door. I was wearing only a towel as I applied my makeup in the tiny bathroom.

"I'll be right there!"

I threw on panties, a bra, and black leggings and then ran to the door. Without checking the peephole first, I opened it—and squealed with joy.

"Chris! What are you doing here?" I flung my arms around his neck.

He lifted me off the ground and whirled us around. Then he kissed my neck. "I wanted to surprise you. I guess I succeeded." He smiled at me.

"Oh yes, you did." I smiled back and kissed his lips.

He kept grinning and stroked my naked back. Goose bumps broke out all over my body.

"Mimi, why are you half-naked? Let's get you inside before your neighbors see you." He hugged me, dragged me into the apartment, and slammed the door.

I giggled. "Hey, that was too loud!"

Christoph held me tighter and slowly pulled me to him until our mouths almost touched. He still wore a sweet smile. "Well, actually I don't care. I like you half-naked," he murmured.

I enjoyed the feel of his rough lips on mine. The stubble on his chin scraped lightly across mine. My heart sped up, quickened by desire, as I closed my eyes and inhaled his aroma. I would have recognized the scent anywhere. I loved the mix of sandalwood soap and his cologne.

"I missed you," I whispered against his chest.

"I missed you more."

He kissed me softly. Our tongues touched, and I dug my hands deep into his blond hair.

"Hey, hey. Slowly, Mimi." He laughed against my mouth and stopped kissing me. He took my hand and led me to a small faded red loveseat, sat down, and pulled me onto his lap. But I sprang back up and moved off, halting a few steps away. He raised his eyebrows.

"I just want to get dressed," I said, gesturing toward the bathroom door behind me.

When I came back, I was wearing my long beige sweater and gray boots. I sat down beside him. "What are you doing here, Christoph?"

"Not much to understand. I wanted to see you, that's all. You don't want me here?"

"Of course." I leaned closer to kiss his cheek. "I'm glad—excited—you're here. I just didn't think I'd see you the first weekend we're apart."

"You're expecting someone else?"

"Actually, yes. I told you about Kriszta. She should be here any minute," I said. "You can come. I'm sure she won't mind. I'm sure we'll have fun exploring the city, the three of us. Or I could just cancel. I hope she doesn't live far. I only know she works in the cafe downstairs." I knew I was rambling, thinking aloud.

"Mia, don't worry," he said and smiled at me. "I found her on Facebook and let her know I was coming to surprise you. After you told me about her, I got in touch with her and asked whether she had any sightseeing tips so that I could show you around. She arranged the tour with you for my sake. I didn't think I'd be here this early, but I didn't want to wait half an hour in front of your door. I had to knock."

I fell on him, arms around his neck, and gave him a kiss. "You are so sweet! Thank you!"

"Oh, I know."

I poked him.

"Let's get going. I have a lot to show you. If I can find everything."

Christoph led me around all the most popular sites. I was so glad I was getting to first see them with him and nobody else.

We strolled down Váci Street. At a fountain we decided to take a breather and sat down on a nearby bench. It was already late afternoon; Chris wouldn't be able to stay overnight because he had class the following day.

"I have to go soon. It's been great seeing you. I can't wait for our next weekend," Chris said, sounding sad.

I gazed deep into his dark chocolate–colored eyes and whispered, "It won't be so long. In two weeks, I'll be home for an entire weekend for Anna's birthday."

We smiled at each other.

"Very soon," I whispered. Chris kissed my forehead and took my hands in his. I looked down at our entwined fingers. I liked the feel of his callused skin. I liked his touch. I felt a blissful warmth flood through me. Chris withdrew one hand, and with his index finger, he tilted up my chin so he could and look into my eyes.

"Mia . . ." He took a deep breath. "Mimi, you are so beautiful."

I bit my lower lip.

"Stop doing that; you'll ruin your lips," he said with his sweetest smile. I stopped chewing immediately. He stroked his thumb over my mouth. "Much better. You know, Mimi, I've thought a lot about us during the past week. I don't like being so far apart." He lowered his gaze briefly, took my other hand again, and continued, "I miss you so much. I don't want you to go away ever again." His face neared. His thigh touched mine. I could feel the heat from his body, and a shiver ran down my spine at the same moment the hair on my arms stood up. "My Mimi. I'm so glad to have you. I never want this to end. OK?"

I could only nod. Tears shot to my eyes and threatened to run down my face.

"Hey, don't cry," he said softly. "This was supposed to be a moment of bliss."

"Only blissful tears," I said quickly.

He looked so happy. He leaned his forehead against mine. Our quickened breaths mingled, sending little steam clouds floating through the winter air around us. He took my face in his hands and stroked my cheeks with his thumbs.

"I love you, Mia!"

My breath caught, and my heart beat loud in my ears. I felt the smile on my face stretch.

"Yes, you heard correctly." He kissed the tip of my nose and repeated, "I love you, Mimi."

"I love you too, Christoph," I answered. I couldn't spill out the words fast enough. My mind and my body were in turmoil. I'd waited so long for this moment, and now it was here. More perfect than I'd imagined. In this wonderful foreign city, as snowflakes swirled around us and the sun tried to break through the clouds, we sealed the memory with a kiss.

"Let's immortalize this moment," he said. He let go of my hands and looked about, searching for something.

"This one here is perfect," he finally said, and showed me the sharp stone he'd picked up. He lowered himself back on the bench and began carving into the wood.

I watched him closely, happily.

"This will be an *M*," he smiled and pressed the stone deeper into the wood. "And now a *C*. And . . . a heart."

I ran my finger along the fresh carvings, then leaned closer and whispered into his ear, "It's amazing." I laid a hand along his cheek to turn his head until we were again looking at each other. "I love you, Christoph."

"I love you too, Mia."

Chapter 15
Mia—You Are Still Here

Budapest, June 2012

Hastily, I threw my backpack over my shoulder and escaped. I had to get away from there fast.

It had been a horrid idea to visit Budapest. *No, no, no . . .*

Feeling a mix of self-pity, rage, and exhaustion, I raced through the maze of narrow streets. My heart pounded against my chest. My lungs burned. I wasn't used to running anymore. Every single muscle in my legs hurt.

Winded, I stopped next to a lamppost, grabbing hold to steady myself. I let my head hang down and tried to regain my breath. My sides ached. I couldn't swallow enough air.

Come on. Calm down.

It was only a memory. A good one that had ultimately ended badly.

Gradually, I managed to steady myself. The ache in my sides subsided, and I straightened. I wiped my forehead with the sleeve of my tunic. There was more than sweat on my face, although I hadn't even noticed I'd also been crying. Christoph didn't deserve any more of my tears. I'd cried enough over him. I dried my cheeks and inhaled deeply.

Only then did I realize where I was. In front of my old apartment. In front of Kriszta's cafe.

Without worrying what memories might haunt me there, I stepped inside.

It smelled exactly like it had in 2009. The same aromas of freshly ground coffee, chocolate cake, and cigars lingered in the air. Nothing had changed.

I sat down at my regular table and twisted around, looking for Kriszta but not seeing her. I skimmed the menu mostly to keep my hands busy, not really reading.

Suddenly I heard a friendly and familiar voice greet me in Hungarian, *"Jó napot!"*

Smiling broadly, I looked up. Kriszta's eyes grew wide. She raced around the table to hug me. I stiffened but told myself I had to endure this. I had to learn how to deal with hugs and handshakes and any sort of touching. Fortunately, the embrace was over quickly, and I let out my breath.

"Oh, Mia!" she shouted. A few patrons looked up. She sat down at my table, almost babbling in her excitement.

"Mia, my dear Mia. I haven't heard from you in such a long time," she said, her speech sweetened by her Hungarian accent. "What brings you to Budapest? Are you staying long? You look so good! Did you cut your hair?" Her words tumbled out. I just watched her and laughed. She hadn't changed. Always cheerful and never quiet.

"OK, I'll shut up now," she said, smiling.

"It's wonderful to see you again, Kriszta," I said quietly.

"Mindjárt jövök," she said, responding to a group at a nearby table, who'd asked for the check. "I'm sorry, but I have to get back to work."

"No worries. I'll wait."

"Like you used to."

"Like I used to." I nodded, and she went back to work. While I waited for her shift to end, she brought me water and my standard large black coffee. She'd remembered.

After she got off, we walked to her apartment.

I settled on her gray, full-grain leather couch while she prepared snacks and drinks.

"I said to make yourself at home, so take off that hat, will you?"

I exhaled slowly through my nose and scratched my neck. Looking at the floor, I shook my head slightly.

"Come on. It's not winter," she said.

Again I shook my head.

"Mia!" she laughed and with a fast movement yanked it off my head. She immediately stopped laughing and stared at me in shock. How I hated those looks. I snatched the gray knit hat out of her hands and put it back on. Kriszta lowered herself next to me. I played nervously with my fingers and, as usual, wanted to scratch my scars.

She nudged me with her shoulder. "You want to talk about it?" she asked gently.

I couldn't—no, *didn't*—want to look at her.

She continued, her voice soft, "Please, Mia. I'll listen. Look at me and talk to me."

Reluctantly, I raised my head and stared straight ahead. Then I shut my eyes and turned toward Kriszta.

"Please," she murmured.

I opened my eyes and looked directly into hers. She waited.

"It happened a little over a year ago," I began. "I didn't feel well. I was sick all the time, until one day I broke down and ended up in the hospital."

Kriszta tried to take my hand, but I snatched it away.

"It's OK. It's only me. Come on. Give me your hand." She showed me the palm of her own. "Put yours on mine. I won't squeeze it or move. Just let it rest there, all right? Try it," she encouraged.

Trembling, I put one hand on my lap. The other shook heavily. I knew Kriszta. I knew she wouldn't hurt me. My hand was only inches from hers. She nodded reassuringly and smiled. Carefully, I moved it closer. My pulse increased at once. I could hear the loud hammering of my heart. Kriszta nodded again, and I placed my hand on her palm. As it rested there, we sat completely still. Kriszta's warmth seeped into my cold fingers. I looked at her, startled. It felt good! She smiled, and my emotions ran wild. I was so proud of myself. I didn't want to remove my hand. I actually wanted to hold hers. I wanted *more*. So I squeezed.

Her grin broadened. "I knew you could do it," she said softly.

I looked at her, overjoyed, then picked up where I'd left off. "I thought I might have a virus, but no." I took a deep breath. "They found a tumor. Actually, two. Both of them malignant. The second was actually a metastasis. The doctor said any day could be my last."

Kriszta had tears in her eyes.

"Please, don't pity me," I said. "I was in the hospital for a long time, and after that, I had chemo. I started losing my hair and emotionally, physically fell into a very bad place. I couldn't understand why all this was happening to me." I stared at our hands. "My whole life went downhill. Christoph broke up with me. He . . . Can you imagine what he did? He left me for Julia, my best friend. Well, not my friend anymore. They hooked up while I was in the hospital."

Kriszta looked at me in shock. "Are you serious?"

I nodded, then smiled a little bit. In hindsight, the whole story was laughable and ridiculous—a cliché.

"It really did me in. You know how much I loved him. I couldn't bear it any longer. I tried to end it all, Kriszta," I whispered.

"You're still here," she replied.

I nodded. "My dad found me in time. Now I'm seeing a therapist, and I'm feeling much better. Just not great. I'm still so sluggish. I can't seem to feel any joy. It's always the same, every day. My therapist told me to leave, go away."

"Away?"

"Well, away from everything familiar—my parents, my hometown. He thinks I need distance. That maybe some physical separation from the past can help me see the beauty of life again."

"You are healed, aren't you?" she asked.

I forced a smile, and she squeezed my hand.

Chapter 16
Samuel—Find Mia

Budapest, June 2012

Eventually I fell asleep, but it was a restless sleep.

In the morning, I stretched and yawned on my way to the bathroom. After a cold shower, I felt better. I wrapped a towel around my hips and searched my backpack for my iPad. I could think about only one thing. Where was she?

I scanned all social-media platforms without any luck. Either she thought they were a waste of time, she wasn't active online, or she had given me a false name.

I would never know.

Damn it . . .

I threw myself on the bed and ran my fingers through my wet hair. This was not how I'd imagined my trip. I wanted to unwind and forget about those beautiful green eyes. But I couldn't, the image of her face refused to leave my thoughts. I had to learn more about Mia. I felt a burning urge to protect her. She seemed so fragile, so vulnerable. Her behavior had aroused my curiosity, leaving me totally confused.

I lay on the bed for a while and eventually got up and dressed. There was not much clothing to choose from. I hadn't been very thoughtful when I'd packed. I opted for my old jeans and a gray shirt.

After a hearty breakfast, I grabbed a coffee to go and explored the city. I visited the Fisherman's Bastion and the Buda Castle, but only the outside. I didn't want to be inside thick, cold walls on such a beautiful day. Buildings fascinated me more from the outside anyway. Then I walked over the Chain Bridge to the other side of town. I was curious to see Váci Street, the famous pedestrian zone. I also needed to buy some more clothes.

I wandered aimlessly, window-shopping, then abruptly stopped. She was there! Just a few yards away, getting up from a bench. It must be her. I recognized her hat from the train.

"Mia!" I shouted, but she didn't respond. She threw her backpack over her shoulder, then rushed toward me. This was my chance.

"Mia Lang," I said in a lowered voice. We were so close, I was certain she'd hear me.

But she only stared straight ahead, hurrying along, even briefly brushing my shoulder before beginning to run.

"Hey, wait!" I yelled and chased after her. She was quick, though. "Hey, Mia, please wait!"

She only ran faster, finally turning to disappear down a narrow side street. I tried hard to follow, but when I rounded the same corner, she was nowhere to be seen.

Damn. I punched a lamppost. I wouldn't get another chance like that again.

I needed to stop obsessing about her. I didn't even know her.

Chapter 17
Mia—A True Friend

Budapest, June 2012

I spent all night at Kriszta's place, and we talked until late into the night. We reminisced about the day we met and all the fun things we'd experienced together. We drank a lot of red wine and giggled like teenagers. It felt good to laugh and talk with someone who didn't eye me awkwardly or pity me. I realized how much I had missed this. The muscles in my cheeks hurt because I had hardly used them the past year. After we'd downed a few glasses, I felt comfortable enough to take off my hat. She smiled, drew her chair closer, and reached for my hand across the table. Her maritime-blue eyes sparkled and I nodded peacefully. She squeezed my fingers.

"I'm so proud of you," she said quietly.

"Thank you," I whispered and looked down. I suddenly felt timid.

"But I have to tell you that your hair is a mess, Mia." Eyes widening, I looked at her. She pressed her lips together, then burst into laughter.

Frowning, I snatched away my hand and crossed my arms over my chest. She wouldn't stop laughing. Well, great for her that I was so entertaining.

"Come on. It was a joke," she said and chuckled. "Short hair looks good on you." I relaxed, and she dried the tears from her cheeks. Then she smiled her broad smile and said, "Seriously, Mia, really good. It's grown in nicely. I can't see any thin spots, like you keep insisting you have. You just need a good cut. Come on." She jumped from her seat and, when she hit her feet, slightly staggered.

"Maybe one glass too many," she muttered, reaching out her hand. I grabbed it, and she lifted me up with one strong pull. "A few pounds more wouldn't harm you, either," she said. I sucked in air. I knew that, but I hadn't regained my desire to eat. I looked at her sadly.

"Don't worry. Your appetite will come back," she said. "Now, follow me." She dragged me to the bathroom and made me sit on the edge of the tub. "Close your eyes."

I did as she asked. "Um . . . what are you doing?"

"Let me surprise you, sweetie. Trust me." I heard her pull something from her pocket, then search through the cabinet.

"Relax," she whispered and combed my hair. Then I heard a metallic sound and—snip!

"Kriszta!" I yelled. She was cutting my hair. "Stop it!"

She just giggled and didn't listen. "Shh. Hold still." She laughed.

"You can barely stand up, so why do you think you can cut my hair?"

"Well, I just can. Now hold still, sweetie," she repeated.

Hold still, I did. She couldn't make things much worse anyway.

"Keep your eyes shut," she demanded. "Get up. Take a few steps forward." She held my elbow and guided me. "Open your eyes," she whispered.

Gingerly, I squinted into the mirror. With my right hand, I ran my fingers through my hair.

"What do you think?" Kriszta asked.

I turned to her. "It actually looks really good. I like it."

"Told you short hair looks good on you. You just needed a serious cut." She grinned from ear to ear.

"Thank you very much," I said and yawned.

"You need a bed for tonight?" she asked.

I nodded.

"You can sleep in mine. That way, you can sleep in."

"That's very generous, but I need to get up early myself. My train leaves at seven."

"You're leaving already?"

"I can't stay here, Kriszta. I've taken care of the thing I most wanted to do—seeing you." We smiled at each other. "But I need to move on, find a place that won't remind me of all the things I want to forget."

"Where are you going?"

"Rome."

"You'll like it. I visited last summer." She pushed me through the bathroom door, back into the living room, and brought me a blanket and pillow. "Bedtime, now. Let's try to get at least two hours of sleep. I'll drop you off at the station on my way to work."

I smiled. "I missed you so much. I'd almost forgotten how much you can say in a single breath."

She nudged my arm and started heading for her room, then turned around and blew me a kiss. "Good night, sweetie. I'll see you in a bit."

Chapter 18
Samuel—Let Coincidence Decide

Budapest, June 2012

After I lost sight of Mia, I took a seat in a small cafe located on the corner where my chase had ended. A young waiter asked me what I wanted. At least I assumed that's what he was saying, but I could only stare at him helplessly. He repeated his question in German, and I ordered a large, strong coffee to keep me awake.

I sat there awhile, and for the first time, I thought seriously about my itinerary. I considered one particular destination, then shied away from it, still haunted by questions—*What would have happened if I had visited her or just answered her calls?* I would never know.

By the time I'd finished my third coffee, I'd decided to cut short my stay in Budapest by a day. I liked this city, but I wanted to make good use of my Eurail pass. I had no clue where I actually wanted to go, though. I opened up my iPad, looked at the rail map, then closed my eyes and moved the cursor until it landed on a random spot. Fate would decide. When I looked again, I saw I was headed to Rome.

I booked a seat online, then rose, paid my check, and continued my walk through the city. I wanted to visit the Great Market Hall, a must-see for every architect. The facade of the basilica-like structure was covered with colorful tiling. Although I usually thought exteriors the most intriguing, this time, I went inside and found the interior to be even more amazing. I didn't know where to start. Delicious aromas wafted from all directions, and my stomach grumbled. I tasted the food at the many different booths, and in the basement, I admired the exotic fish filling huge tanks. Of course, there were also souvenir shops to browse.

The day sped by. I ended up spending all afternoon in the market, which was well worth the time.

Outside, I hailed a cab and returned to the hotel. I ordered room service for dinner, ate, then went to bed early. I had a long train ride ahead of me the following day.

My alarm went off at five. I fumbled for the smart phone on my nightstand, hit snooze, and rolled onto my belly, hiding my head under the pillow. I'd never been an early bird, and here I'd booked a seat on a train departing at seven in the morning. Great. Five minutes later, the alarm sounded again. *All right, all right. Getting up now.* My eyes were still half-closed, but I sat up, yawned loudly, rubbed my eyes, and ran both my hands through my sleep-mussed hair. The alarm went off a third time. Goddamn phone. I was now wide-awake.

After a few minutes in the bathroom, I was ready. I hurried as I didn't want to miss the train. I ate a quick breakfast at the hotel—and ended up arriving at the station an hour early. Whatever. I decided to get some coffee and relax on one of the platform benches.

A cup of coffee in one hand and my guitar in the other, I searched for the right platform, found it, spotted a bench—and also spotted someone I knew. My heart pounding fast, I sat down beside her.

"Good morning, Mia."

"Oh . . . shit, you totally scared me!" She took her earbuds out and looked at me, her expression weary. I couldn't say she seemed happy to see me again.

"Sorry, I didn't mean to." I brushed some strands of hair from my forehead. "I thought you'd likely notice when someone sat down next to you," I added dryly.

She inhaled deeply, still studying me. "No worries," she whispered. That voice, that voice whispering . . . It drove me crazy.

"Just don't do it again," she said coolly. She turned away and plugged in her earbuds again. She scrolled through her iPhone, likely selecting music, and then leaned back. Eyes closed. Arms crossed over her chest.

Chapter 19
Mia—You Are Still Yourself

Budapest, June 2012

"Mia, come on. Get up!"

Kriszta stood next to the couch. She was already dressed, her makeup done, holding a cup of coffee.

I rubbed my eyes. I was so tired, and the ceiling lamp was glaring.

"Turn out . . . the . . . light, please," I murmured hoarsely.

Kriszta laughed. "Nope, the light stays on. It's almost five o'clock. Get up, sleepyhead." Kriszta was surprisingly wide-awake and cheerful after only two hours of sleep. I couldn't understand it. Especially when I considered all the wine we'd had. My head felt like it was filled with cotton.

"Come on, Mia. I want to drop you off at the station, but I have to be at work at half past six."

"OK, OK," I groaned.

"Good girl." She smiled, and I shook my head. Ouch . . . Not a good idea with this headache. "What's wrong?" she asked

"I don't get how you can be up and bubbly after so little sleep," I managed to say, yawning and shuffling behind her into the kitchen. "And look at you. Like, no dark circles, immaculate skin, perfectly groomed and dressed. I mean, you look far too good for two hours, *two hours* of sleep."

Kriszta grinned from ear to ear.

"Yes, I meant that as a compliment, so go ahead and gloat," I said while she poured me a cup of coffee. I held the mug with both hands, enjoying the aroma of fresh-brewed espresso.

"Nice outfit, by the way," I murmured. "The pale pink shorts and beige blouse look great on you."

"Thanks. Now hurry up. Finish your coffee, get dressed, and let's go."

I was still tired when I crawled into Kriszta's old Toyota Starlet after tossing my backpack in the backseat.

"This old thing is still alive?" I said and fastened my seat belt.

"Whoa! Careful—be nice to her, or she won't drive you to the station." She patted the dashboard. "Though I wouldn't mind keeping you here longer."

"I really can't stay, Kriszta," I said quietly. "Yesterday was amazing, but I don't feel good here, you know?" Where *did* I feel good?

"I know. And I want you to feel better. Mia, you're still yourself." She looked at me and reached for my hand. This time, I flinched. Yesterday I had been courageous, fueled by the wine. But today I couldn't let her touch me.

Staring at my feet, I murmured, "Please look at me." I raised my head and met her sparkling eyes. "I don't know how to live like this. Everything I had was taken away. Life is such a struggle now. A fight."

Kriszta exhaled deeply and shook her head. "You can't think that way. Take joy in everything you've already achieved." She smiled. "Because you've already made it. You're still here." She added quietly, "Always remember that."

I didn't answer. I turned to look out the window. She started the engine and drove to the station.

In the parking lot, she stopped and got out of the car. I waited a moment, breathing evenly, then grabbed my backpack.

"I can't come inside with you. I need to leave directly for work."

I nodded.

"Mia, you'll be yourself again. In fact, you still *are* yourself. I saw it yesterday. I saw your laughter, your real laughter. You can do this."

"Thank you," I said in a low voice. I didn't know how to handle these motivational speeches, no matter who said them—Kriszta, Dr. Weiß, my parents. On one hand, they made me feel better, because people believed in me. On the other hand, I was terrified I'd fail. What if I never again found my old passion for life to drive me forward once more? How long could I encourage myself to continue on? How long would I last?

I trembled, then offered her an open hand, palm up. My heart was beating fast. Her hand rested in mine, and she held on for a long time.

"I'll miss you. Please let's keep in touch. Let me know when you get to Rome."

There was a lump in my throat when I let go. I slung my backpack over my shoulder, waved good-bye to my friend, and walked toward the station.

Chapter 20
Mia—Just Tune Out

Budapest, June 2012

I searched for my cell phone and earbuds in the pockets of my backpack. This thing was too large—or I was too dense—because it seemed I could never quickly find anything I was looking for.

I squatted in front of the station and emptied the entire side pocket. I heard passersby swear under their breaths. The words might be Hungarian, but I had learned at least that much of the language when I'd lived here. Maybe I was in their way, with my stuff spilled out around me, but I needed music. Now. I needed to tune out.

Once I found what I wanted, I hastily crammed everything else back in, walked inside, and headed directly to the platform. Once there, I got comfortable on a bench and would have dozed off had it not been for a male voice.

"Good morning, Mia."

My eyes flew open. My knees began trembling, and my pulse sped up.

"Oh . . . shit, you totally scared me!" I looked at Samuel, feeling weary. He must be stalking me. Showing up like this couldn't be sheer coincidence. I turned away and blew out a long breath to calm myself.

Samuel immediately apologized. I looked back at him in acknowledgment, but I didn't feel like talking. He ran his fingers through his hair and wet his lower lip, a gesture that stirred some very interesting feelings. What was wrong with me? I couldn't stand him. But his physical perfection made it damn hard not to think about certain things.

I gulped in a mouthful of air, hoping to distract myself from my thoughts. "No worries," I whispered. I just hoped he wouldn't do anything to set my mind on that course again.

I plugged in my earbuds and chose some soothing tunes. Then I tucked the cell phone back in my pocket and closed my eyes.

An announcement sounded. I reached to silence the music and waited for the broadcast to be repeated in English.

"Due to technical difficulties, the train from Budapest to Vienna will be delayed for approximately thirty minutes."

Bummer. I looked at my watch. That really meant waiting another forty-five minutes.

"That sucks," Samuel said as he played with his empty coffee cup, running his index finger along the brim.

I stared at the floor.

"Would you like a coffee? I'll get you one," he offered.

Without meeting his eyes, I shook my head and followed the movement of his fingers. It was easier than looking into his big gray eyes.

"OK, your choice. I'm getting another cup. It will be a long ride to Rome. Would you mind watching my stuff?"

I looked at him, terrified. Seriously? He was going to Rome, like me? Panic shot through my body. The blood raced through my veins, and my palms grew damp. My stomach ached, and a strange weakness flooded my body, down to my knees and my toes. I wanted peace, serenity. I didn't want Samuel Winter tagging along, following me everywhere, all across Europe.

I quickly closed my eyes before I could look at him again and concentrated on my breathing, trying to fend off another panic attack. I clenched my hands into fists, my nails drilling into my flesh, deeper and deeper. I took more breaths. Gradually, I managed to relax them, moving my stiff fingers.

"Is everything OK?" Samuel asked.

OK . . . OK . . . OK . . . No, nothing is OK.

Hesitantly, I nodded and opened my eyes.

"Would you mind watching my stuff?" he asked again. With his chin, he gestured toward his backpack. I nodded slightly, and he walked away.

A few minutes later, he was back.

"I wasn't sure how you like your coffee," he said. I raised my eyebrows at him. He was grinning. "I decided I'd bring you a cup anyway, but I didn't know what you'd want, so I have a cappuccino, a latte, an espresso with cold milk, and a double espresso. Take your pick."

He tapped his right foot, his eyebrows raised.

"Black, strong, and large, please," I said timidly.

Samuel put down the other three cups and, with both his hands, handed me the large espresso. It would be difficult to avoid touching him. I grasped the cup near the lid. Slowly, he let go.

"Thank you," I said. "How much do I owe you?"

"My treat." He smiled.

I took a careful sip but still burned my lips. "Shit."

"Oh crap. Did you hurt yourself?" He was getting on my nerves. I stood up, leaving the cup on the bench.

"Could you . . . ?"

He raised his face to me. He wasn't smirking anymore. I looked directly into his eyes. Their gray hue reminded me of the sky on a dark, rainy day, streaked with traces of light where the sun struggles to break through thick clouds.

"Yes?" He held my gaze.

I swallowed and tried to form my words without stammering again. It didn't work. "Could you also—um—keep an eye on my things?"

"Sure." He smiled.

I gave him my fake grin in return and then headed to the bathroom.

I was drying my hands when, in the mirror, I saw a man appear directly behind me, a disgusting sneer on his dirty face. His teeth, the few he had, were yellow. His clothes were old, filthy, and ragged.

Dread rose inside me. I grasped the edge of the sink. We stared at each other in the mirror.

Both hands in his pockets, he took a step closer. My heart hammered, and I could hear a rushing in my ears. Another step. I spun around but had to grab the sink again to keep from falling. I had to get out of here.

Carefully, hands still behind me, I felt along the sink, trying not to make any quick moves. He stepped along with me, shaking his head.

"What do you want?" I whispered, my voice hoarse with fear.

He didn't answer. He only stared. I was in a sheer panic and panting roughly.

Reaching the tiled wall, I pressed my back against it and slowly slid toward the exit. A few yards more, and I would be able to touch the doorknob. I could make it. I trembled and lunged the final few feet.

The man moved just as fast. He caught me and pressed me against the tiles. He reeked of alcohol, cigarette smoke, and vomit. I would have thrown up had there been anything in my stomach to lose.

"*Csinos teremtés,*" he breathed into my face.

His hands wandered down my body and stopped at my belly.

I squeezed my eyes shut.

Chapter 20 ½
Mia—Don't Touch Me

Graz, January 2012

"Mia, are you here?" I heard Dr. Weiß's voice and felt his finger on my wrist, taking my pulse. "You're calming down," he said softly. "Open your eyes slowly. You are in my office."

My eyes fluttered, and eventually, I managed to keep them open.

"Inhale deeply. You've just come around," he said.

I was lying on his big leather couch. Dr. Weiß was kneeling on the ground beside it. I tried to sit up, but he gently pushed me back.

"Wait another minute." He stood up and brought me a glass of water.

I reached out, but I was trembling so much I would have spilled the water one-handed. I had to use both. I struggled up a little so I could drink more easily. After three big gulps, the glass was empty. I handed it back to Dr. Weiß.

"Would you like more?" he asked.

I nodded. I downed the next glass in the same record speed and finally sat up straight.

"Do you want to tell me what happened?" Dr. Weiß asked. I could see he was concerned.

"Dr. Weiß, I—I know . . . I think . . ." I exhaled. "I don't know. I don't even know how I ended up on this couch."

I scratched at my scars. I hated these blackouts, which gripped me seemingly every other second. Whenever I came to, I'd find myself in a completely different setting.

"You stormed into my office. You were very distraught," he said. "What happened?"

I squeezed my eyes shut and shook my head. I hadn't come to talk about what'd made me so angry. I'd come because I knew it was the only place I could find the serene environment I so desperately needed.

"You still don't want to talk?" He massaged his forehead and scratched his beard. It was apparent he didn't know how to help me, either. "You know, Mia"—he paused and looked at me—"I understand you don't like to talk about your *things*, as you call them. But you need to realize I am not your enemy."

He paced the room, ten steps in one direction, ten steps in the opposite, hands clasped behind his back. He paused again, a few feet away from me.

"You're your own enemy," he said. "Yes, Mia. You want to reconcile with the world, but before you can do that, you need to reconcile with yourself. You need to allow emotions. Right now, the only adversary you are confronting is you." I opened my mouth to respond, but he continued without stopping, "You can tell me another hundred times that you are OK, but I still won't believe you."

He sat down on a corner of the small coffee table and leaned forward. "You need to talk with me," he said in a friendly yet determined tone.

He was right. I was standing in my own way. Maybe I should accept his help. Doctors weren't my foes. They wanted to help me.

"OK," I whispered.

"Good." He smiled. "And now we'll revisit the beginning of our session step-by-step. We need to find the triggers for your panic attacks."

I nodded.

"So, you stormed through the door and ran right to me. Your expression changed, and you began screaming. I couldn't get through to you. I brought you to the sofa. Is there anything you remember? Why did you scream?"

I took a deep breath. "I had a bad day. I knew I could find some quiet here."

"I'm glad you feel comfortable here, Mia." With a brief nod, he motioned for me to go on.

"I ran into you. Your hand touched my belly, and that's all I remember."

"I see. What else happened today?" He didn't ask any further questions about my blackout.

I scratched my scar.

He watched my fingers. "Please stop doing that." He then walked to his desk, grabbed a black leather notebook, and handed it to me. "Write about everything that makes you do that. Much better than scratching. Give your arm a break."

He asked me to continue.

With a trembling voice, I said, "I had th-the exam today. They looked at everything. I was so scared." Tears shot to my eyes. "One of the doctors wanted to see the scar." I pointed at my belly. "I screamed. I don't know why. The doctor tried to reassure me. He said he only wanted to see if the stitches had healed well. He touched me, and I felt like I was under attack or something. I—I was afraid he wanted to cut me open again. He couldn't calm me down. A nurse had to come and grab my arms so that he could look at the incision." Tears streamed down my face. "Then they let me go. It took forever until I had myself under control again."

"Thank you for sharing this. I'm proud of you."

I looked at the floor and bit my lower lip. He was proud of me.

"Smile, Mia. That was a very good beginning."

Chapter 21
Samuel—Come Back

Budapest, June 2012

Mia had been gone for longer than fifteen minutes, and I began to worry, even though she still had her backpack here. She wouldn't just split without her stuff. Even with that self-reassurance, my anxiety grew, and I tapped my right foot while looking up and down the platform. She was nowhere to be seen.

I had to do something. I grabbed both our backpacks and headed toward the restrooms. On my way, I continued to scan the station's main hall but saw no sign of her.

I picked up my pace and reached the women's restroom. I tore open the door. "Mia?" I called. No answer. I ran back to the platform to see whether she'd returned to the bench while I was gone. No Mia.

I spun around and spotted another women's restroom. I ran to it as quick as I could, and this time I found her, lying on the floor. I tossed our luggage and my guitar into the corner and kneeled beside her. She looked terrible—ashen and lifeless. But her chest was moving, and I could feel her pulse racing. What had happened?

I lifted her up a bit. I didn't want to leave her on the cold, dirty tiles. She fought me, so I let go of her once she was in a sitting position. I gently checked her pulse again. It had slowed, I thought.

"Mia, are you with me?" I asked her quietly when I noticed rapid movement under her eyelids. She opened her eyes and looked at me, her expression confused and scared. She immediately pulled away.

I lifted both arms, palms out, surrender-style, and said, "Everything is OK, Mia. I was looking for you." I moved closer, but she waved a hand, clearly a gesture telling me to stay away. "All right, I won't come closer. Do you want to tell me what happened?"

She shook her head. She looked so frightened.

I reached to my backpack in the corner, pulled out a bottle of water, and handed it to her. "Here, drink, please." She did, voraciously, as if she hadn't had a drop in days. Shuddering, she returned the half-empty container to me.

"Thank you," she whispered, staring at her feet.

"Look at me, just briefly, please. I want to see how you're doing." Reluctantly, she raised her head, and I dove into the emerald sea of her eyes. I saw tears and fear there.

"What happened?" I repeated.

"I . . . I must not have been feeling well. No breakfast, forgot to eat."

I could tell by the tension in her body and jaw that she wasn't telling the truth, but I didn't want her defenses rising any more than they already were by pressing further. So I just nodded and let it go for the time being.

"Well, the most important thing is that I found you." I stood and grabbed our luggage. "Let's go. We have a train to catch." I extended my hand to help her up, but she hid hers behind her back and smiled at me. She didn't do false smiles very well, I'd noticed.

She heaved herself to her feet. Her legs were trembling, and I wanted to steady her, but she grabbed the sink before I could. I gave her a worried glance. She didn't look at me. Instead, she stared at the ground.

"It's OK," she managed to say and reached out her hand. "Give me my backpack." I did as she asked. "Thank you." She took a deep breath and finally looked me in the eye. Her expression was much calmer now. "Thank you for coming to find me."

"Of course."

We walked to the platform in silence. I decided that from now on, I would always watch over her. It was clear she wasn't doing well, although she was apparently trying to convince me and the rest of the world otherwise. Her body language indicated that. And she was a terrible liar.

"Hold on a second. I'll get us new coffees," Mia said. We walked over to the coffee bar, and she searched her pockets for some cash.

"Don't worry about it." I pulled out some bills. "It's only coffee."

I received another whispered "Thank you."

We arrived just as the train was approaching the platform. Mia boarded first and chose a window seat. I waited, watching her settle in. Then I asked, "Do you mind if I sit with you?" She eyed me, then bit her lower lip. Man, she looked sexy.

"Well, what are you waiting for?" She nodded to the seat across from her.

That didn't sound too inviting.

Chapter 22
Mia—Together

En route to Rome, June 2012

Exhausted, I threw myself onto my seat. I took off my shoes and plugged my earbuds in. At that moment, I couldn't care less that he was sitting directly across from me. I was still in shock after the incident in the restroom. I'd suffered similar ones, the last earlier in the year. I hadn't known until I'd sorted things out with my therapist that they were triggered by touching the scar on my belly. That's why nobody was allowed to come near the incision. Sometimes, though, like in the restroom, I couldn't stop it.

Maybe my phobia had rescued me from a worse assault. The creep had vanished when my knees gave in and I hit the floor. My head still throbbed, and I could feel a lump growing. The last thing I'd seen before shock paralyzed me was the guy's legs as he hurried out the door. Then everything had gone dark.

Samuel Winter, of all people, had found me. I really had to reconsider my opinion about him. He was uberfriendly. If that'd been all he was, that would be one thing. But he was also so attractive. More and more, I caught myself peeking at him in order to memorize every feature on his gorgeous face.

When I'd realized it was him kneeling next to me on the restroom floor, I'd had to put more distance between us. But not before inhaling his scent. It reminded me of fresh forest air. Thinking about it, in spite of myself, I felt the corners of my lips turn up.

"What are you smiling about?" His deep voice sounded through the music, startling me. I flinched and almost fell off my seat. Angrily, I paused my iPhone and looked at him.

"Um . . . well, sorry." He grinned.

I enjoyed his company. I didn't know why, but I could talk with him without fear of a panic attack.

"Damn it. Don't do that," I said in a voice halfway between yelling and whispering.

"Won't happen again," he said, trying not to laugh.

I straightened my back and crossed my feet. "That's what you said last time."

He smirked. "So you really won't tell me what made you smile?" He leaned forward and pointed at my mouth. "It looked good on you."

I inwardly cursed my heated cheeks. "Well, I was just thinking about something. Not really important," I snapped. I motioned to my earbuds to signal I wasn't interested in further chitchat. He nodded, leaned back, and took out his own earbuds.

Samuel Winter didn't seem at all like I'd imagined him.

On the way to Vienna, we each remained lost in our own thoughts. Mine involved him. I wasn't sure whether I wanted to continue to Rome if it meant traveling with him. I kept glancing across the space between us. Our eyes met several times, each one making me smile. Eventually, I nodded off.

Shortly before the train arrived in Vienna, I heard his voice. "Hey, sweetie." I opened my eyes and looked directly into his. He squatted in front of me. "I promised I wouldn't scare you again," he whispered. Enchanted, I stared into his face, his looks continuing to fascinate me much more than I thought was wise.

"I wasn't sure you'd heard the announcement. We'll be arriving shortly."

I wrapped the earbud cable around the iPhone and stowed it in the side pocket of my backpack.

"Thanks. No, I didn't hear it." I put on my shoes and zipped up my bag. The train rolled slowly into the station. Samuel stood and held out his hand. I didn't want to give him any more reasons to think I was crazy, so this time I ignored the impulse to hide my hand behind my back. But I was still afraid he might touch me. He was far too close. I simply said, "Thanks, I'll be OK."

"All right. But let me carry your pack." He held his hand out, waiting for me to give it to him.

"No worries. I can carry my own stuff. Plus, you have your guitar."

The train jolted to a halt, and I started toward the exit.

"Hey, Mia, wait up!" he called as I jumped down the steps. At the sound of his voice, I stopped short, stood stiffly, and waited until he caught up. "We're headed the same way. Let's go together."

There it was. I had been pondering how to handle this since we'd left Budapest. I wanted to be alone. Rediscover myself without anybody else around. Begin to like myself again. Do the things I'd once loved or had always wanted to try. I wavered, hesitating mostly because I liked his company. Maybe I didn't need to be alone. He wasn't a part of my past anyway.

He scratched his head. "OK, it was just a thought. Since we have the same destination and everything, I thought it might be fun."

Before thinking any more about it—I'd certainly done more than my share of thinking over the past year—I said, "Sure. Why not?" I hoped I wasn't making a mistake. His endless attempts to strike up a conversation had already gotten on my nerves.

"Well then, let's go. We have half an hour to get to Westbahnhof to catch the train to Rome."

Maybe it was naive of me to allow him access into my world. But what was there to lose, anyway?

Chapter 23
Samuel—I Quit

En route to Rome, June 2012

"Samuel..."

It was the first time I'd heard her say my name. I liked how she said it.

"Slow down, please." She was out of breath.

I stopped and waited for her. "Sorry, just a habit. Here, give me your backpack." I held out my hand.

She shook her head.

"Please?"

She rolled her eyes, then handed it to me. "Fine, if it makes you feel better."

"Hell, yes, it does." I lifted the heavy thing and grinned. "Let's go. Rome is waiting."

People were already boarding the train when we arrived at the platform at Westbahnhof. As soon as we'd stepped on, the train departed.

"Without you, I would have missed it." Mia plopped down on a seat. "I don't know Vienna at all. It would have taken me an hour to get here."

"Home advantage." I put down our luggage. Mia pulled her iPhone from her bag, but before she could plug up her ears again, I asked, "Why are you traveling by yourself?"

Again, she bit her lower lip. And again, man, it looked sexy. She shrugged and held my gaze with her sparkling eyes. Then she leaned back and, with her arms crossed over her chest, asked, "Why are you not in your office, *Samuel Winter*?"

I sat back myself and ran my fingers through my hair. "You know who I am?"

She nodded slowly.

"What exactly do you know?" I tried to hide my emotions. I didn't want to be reminded of my father or his company.

"More than I'd like."

"Is that the reason you've been avoiding me?" I was sick and tired of my dad's damned architecture firm. It caused me only headaches and haunted me everywhere I went, even here, when all I wanted was to escape my past.

"Partly," she answered.

"How did you find out?" I hadn't even been aware of my father's wrongdoings. Maybe I really had hidden from the truth.

"I used to work for a newspaper. I don't understand how you could lend your face to something like that. You're considered the hotshot of the real estate scene." She shook her head. "I really don't get it." Then she added more amicably, "Especially now that I've come to know you a little bit. It doesn't make sense."

I leaned forward and looked directly into her eyes. "I had no idea what was going on," I said warily. She frowned. "My father didn't involve me in the business end. I wasn't a project manager. I usually only sat at my desk and designed for him."

"That's hard to believe," she snapped.

"It's the truth," I replied. "I left the firm. I'm sure he's struggling to come up with an explanation as to why his famous *hotshot* son has gone cold."

She still didn't seem convinced. "You're serious?"

"Absolutely serious. I quit. My father had just assigned me my first project to spearhead. When I read through the documents, I discovered his dirty secret. Well, apparently it's not even that much of a secret. Everybody but me seems to have known." I ran my fingers through my hair. "We had a bad falling out. I'll never go back there."

"Not everybody knows," Mia said quietly. "We—me and the newspaper staff—found out only by accident. And then your father discovered we knew. We couldn't go public. He would have sued us to death."

"What a prick," I spat.

"I'm glad you finally got it. I would've been disappointed . . . you know, if you were a part of all that." Mia peeked at me. She smiled and bit her lower lip. She had to stop doing that. Didn't she realize she was torturing me?

"So why Eurail?" she said, interrupting my thoughts. "Why not a private jet, maybe?" I loved the sound of her giggle.

"There is no private jet." I laughed, then sighed and added, "I had to get away from home. And not just because of what happened professionally."

She nodded. Her eyes displayed a sadness that conveyed she understood exactly what I meant.

Chapter 24
Samuel—Connected Through Music

En route to Rome, June 2012

Mia yawned and covered her mouth with her hand. "I'm really sorry. I'd love to go on talking, especially now that you've told me everything." I was glad we'd had a frank talk and that my dad's firm's reputation wasn't standing between us anymore. Mia smiled at me. A different smile, a real one. A smile that didn't seek to chase me away.

She seemed barely able to keep her eyes open. "I'm so tired. I visited an old friend last night, and we didn't get to bed till really late."

"Go on and sleep. We have a long way until Rome." She wouldn't slip away again. She was actually speaking to me, voluntarily. And I wanted to hear more.

Performing her usual routine, she grabbed her iPhone, put in her earbuds, leaned back, and closed her eyes. We had hours to go before we arrived in Italy's capital. Hours I would spend in Mia's company—or, at least, hours I would sit next to her and watch her.

She opened her eyes. Confused, she inspected her phone, then pushed several buttons.

"What's wrong?" I asked.

She stuffed the device back into her bag and grumbled, "Battery's dead."

I laughed, but she frowned. "What's so funny?" she asked.

"I'm not laughing at you." I raised my hands, as if fending her off. "I would offer you mine, but my battery is dead, too." She grinned. "I told you I wasn't laughing at you." I winked at her.

"Hmm, bummer."

"No big deal," I said. "You can charge it in a few hours." She nodded and began to bite her nails, then stopped when she realized I was watching and instead picked at a cuticle. Something was bugging her.

"Is it important for you to listen to music?" I asked.

"Actually, yeah."

"Why?"

Mia just stared at me. She opened her mouth as if she intended to speak, then closed it and chewed her lower lip again. I was instantly charmed.

"OK, no answer. I get it. But if it's that serious, I could play something for you."

Her eyes grew wide, and she stopped biting her lip. "Really?"

I shrugged. "Why not? We need to pass the time somehow." A smile broke across her face, and then she laughed. I liked how her emerald eyes sparkled when she was happy like this. Our gazes caught and held. Her aroma wafted toward me . . . a subtle whiff of vanilla . . .

Softly, I asked, "Do you play an instrument?"

"I used to," she answered quietly.

"Not anymore?"

"I haven't played in over a year." She looked down at her fidgety fingers.

"Why? What did you play?"

She massaged her neck with her right hand. "I . . . um . . ." She drew air in and out a few times, then finally said, "I just didn't have time anymore."

Her behavior was puzzling. A simple question about the instrument she played had eclipsed her happiness in an instant.

The artificial smile was back. Before I could dig deeper, she said, "So, then, show me what you can do."

"Any requests?"

"No. Play whatever you like. Whatever you play best. Anything." She nestled into her seat, closed her eyes, then opened them again. "Thank you," she said, lips curving again.

"My pleasure."

I unpacked my guitar, quickly tuned it, then played random melodies, anything that popped into my head.

I had been playing for an hour and thought she was asleep. Her breathing was even, and she was still. I'd just gotten into "Staring at the Sky" when I noticed she was singing along under her breath. I was already stirred by the throaty way she talked, but hearing her sing gave me goose bumps. Her voice was magnificent.

I chimed in on the second strophe. Immediately, she stopped. Her eyes flew open, and she covered her mouth, obviously embarrassed. I continued to play the melody and said, "I didn't expect you to know this song."

She didn't say a word. Her face was ashen.

"Breathe, sweetie. Your voice is great. I love it."

Her hands dropped to her lap. I put the guitar aside and motioned for her to continue her relaxation technique. She struggled for a moment. Then she looked into my eyes and calmed down.

"You all right now?" I was worried.

"Y-yes, OK," she stammered. "I-I didn't realize I was singing along."

"But you should sing along! You have a great voice." She blushed. "Come on, let's do it some more."

"No, really, Samuel, I shouldn't." She was being evasive again.

"Oh please, Mia, just this one song. Then I'll stop bugging you." I hoped my smile would convince her, but she just shook her head. I reached to take one of her hands, but she tucked them behind her. Why did she do that all the time?

"Come on, Mia. One song. You'll like it. I know it."

She thought for a moment, then threw me a timid glance.

"OK, but just this one."

Chapter 25
Mia—May I Touch?

En route to Rome, June 2012

Why did I agree to sing with him? I'd abandoned all this a year ago. My piano had been gathering dust in the living room since April 2011, just like so many other things I'd once liked. I'd always enjoyed singing when I was sure nobody was listening. Once I got out of the hospital, though, I was too tired for it. My joints were too stiff to play. I didn't take joy in it anymore. Until that day on the train, I hadn't even felt the urge to do more than listen.

Joining in felt so natural that I hadn't even noticed when it happened. Maybe because I was only half-awake, with the guitar lulling me to sleep. I might not have even caught on at all, if Samuel's crooning hadn't startled me into it. He sang very well. I stopped because our voices melded so perfectly.

It felt good.

Too good. This kind of feeling wasn't familiar anymore. It overwhelmed me, and I didn't know how to handle my emotions. They scared me. For more than a year, I had been living inside a bubble and unable to find the exit. I was going in circles. Then suddenly, the bubble burst, because of one moment, one person? That scared me. But I had to fight and find my way out.

So I sang, too.

I enjoyed the sound of his voice; it made my skin tingle. I liked what I felt inside—warmth, happiness. I could only manage the one tune for now. I didn't want to be overcome by my feelings.

"Thank you for joining in." Samuel smiled. I looked at him shyly. "We should do this more often. I would love to see that smile again, the one that happens when you sing."

"Another time, maybe . . ." I couldn't say anything else.

Samuel kept playing for me until I finally fell asleep. I simply couldn't keep my eyes open any longer, although I really wanted to listen some more.

He woke me shortly before the train crossed the Italian border. I was grateful he didn't touch me. He simply repeated my name. "Mia, wake up . . . Mia Lang, time to open those gorgeous eyes of yours. Mia . . ."

I pretended to be asleep because I wanted to listen to Samuel say my name. I didn't move a muscle, but eventually, I couldn't suppress my smile.

"Hey, how long have you been awake?" he asked. He was so close I could feel his breath on my face. Slowly, I opened my eyes. He was really, really near, our noses separated by maybe four inches. Exciting sensations and a long-missing warmth ran through my body.

"Um . . . maybe a little while?" I said softly.

"Then why did you pretend you were sleeping?" His face was still close.

I shrugged.

He shook his head. "Whatever. We'll have to get off the train soon. I'll grab your backpack again because we don't have much time for the transfer."

"But I can—"

"I'm taking it. Period. We only have five minutes."

"OK, OK, you take it." I rolled my eyes and covered my mouth to indicate I was shutting up.

"Ready? Let's go, pronto!"

We were traveling the next leg of our trip by bus. After we'd boarded, I stowed my pack under my seat and rested my knees against the back of the one in front of me. Samuel took the spot beside me. The bus was fully booked and cramped.

"Do you mind if I sleep a little more?" I asked.

Samuel shook his head. "I'll try to rest a bit myself."

"OK. So, I'll see you in Venice, if not before." I yawned.

"Sleep well, sweetie."

This was the third time he'd called me sweetie. I thought I'd heard wrong the first times. Now I wanted to ask him why he kept using an endearment. But he'd already closed his eyes, his arms crossed over his chest. His legs were far too long for the narrow space. One leg was buckled up against the seat in front of him and the other stretched into the aisle. A small smile played on his face; his breathing was even. I still enjoyed looking at him. It was soothing and exciting at the same time. For more than a year, I hadn't been this close to a man. I wanted to touch him so much that my hands began to tingle. I shifted and extended my arm until my fingertips almost brushed his face. But I hesitated—then I told myself he was sleeping and couldn't do me any harm.

Softly, I caressed his short beard, then quickly withdrew my hand. Only to try it again. Briefly, gently, I touched his mouth with my trembling fingers. His lips were softer than my skin. I smiled. I liked their texture. Then he stirred, and I drew back again.

Pleased with myself, I settled back in my seat. I was still smiling when I drifted off to sleep.

Chapter 26
Mia—Don't Touch Me

En route to Rome, June 2012

I woke up with a stiff neck. I couldn't wait to lie down on a real bed, even if it was in a youth hostel. It would definitely be more comfortable than sleeping on a cramped bus, leaning against the window.

I stretched all my aching limbs as best as I could, yawned, and looked at my watch. It was almost six in the evening. Any minute, we would arrive in Venice, where we'd catch another transfer for the final leg to Rome.

I glanced over at Samuel, who was still fast asleep. His head hung down so awkwardly, I figured he'd have a stiff neck, as well.

I leaned over to whisper in his ear. "Samuel, wake up. We're almost there. Time to get up, Samuel Winter."

He opened one eye and peeked at me.

"We'll have to get off the bus soon."

He yawned and stretched. "Damn it. I didn't imagine traveling would be so painful."

"What did you think? Luxury coaches?"

He laughed. "No, I must have just forgotten how uncomfortable these seats are." He massaged his neck.

"Once we're back on a train, we can spread out more, and we won't be nearly on top of each other," I said.

"Yeah, but what if I like being nearly top of each other?" he asked, stretching as if to reach around my shoulders and hug me.

I hastily pressed myself against the side of the bus. Blood rushed through my veins, making my heart race. This was just too much.

Sam raised his hands in that surrender gesture again. "Hey, sweetie, relax. It was only going to be a hug." I heard his voice but couldn't speak. A swooshing noise filled my ears, making my head throb. I couldn't avert my eyes away from his damned hands.

"Mia, please, look into my eyes," he said. "I won't hurt you."

I knew he wouldn't. But my body didn't agree. My body thought he was an enemy, and every cell had retreated into defense mode. I had to do something, or I'd have another panic attack.

"Look into my eyes."

Carefully, I raised my eyes.

"Now, try to breathe. Just do as I do."

But I couldn't. I felt as if I were choking. I squeezed my eyes shut.

"No, Mia, look into my eyes," he repeated gently.

I forced myself to do as he asked.

"Good . . . Inhale . . . and now, slowly, exhale. In . . ." He pointed up. "And out . . ." He pointed down. We repeated the exercise over twenty times, until the rushing in my head disappeared and my heartbeat slowed.

"Good job," Samuel said, smiling at me. Sounding tentative, as if choosing his words carefully, he said, "If you don't mind my asking, what happened?"

I shook my head.

"I think I deserve to know, don't you? I thought you'd faint any minute. You scared me."

I didn't want him to think I was even crazier than he must believe I was already. More than that, I didn't want to stir up anything painful. If I explained my panic attacks, I'd have to tell him the whole story.

"I can't, Samuel. I mean, I'd rather not. Besides, it's no big deal."

He seemed to debate whether or not he should push me. He ran his fingers through his disheveled hair, massaged his neck. Looked at me. Looked away.

"OK, I'll let it go. For now." His voice betrayed his confusion. My eyes begged him to forget about it. "I'll let it go only because we're transferring soon."

"Thank you," I whispered and looked at the ground.

Chapter 27
Samuel—Never Let Go Again

En route to Rome, June 2012

I couldn't wrap my head around her behavior. It worried me. Her reactions weren't normal. How could I get her to confide in me? We hardly knew each other, although it seemed as if we'd known each other forever, which, of course, wasn't the case. If it were, I would have known what was going on with her and been able to help. She seemed so fragile and scared, but she obviously didn't want me to know why, so I let the subject drop.

When the bus stopped, I grabbed her luggage. This time, she didn't protest and instead simply thanked me. Even without the heavy backpack, she moved slowly.

In silence, we boarded the train to Rome. Suddenly, Mia stopped and looked at me, doubt in her eyes.

"What's the matter?" I asked.

"I don't want you to think I'm crazy. I . . ." She began chewing her lower lip again. I wanted to smooth her mouth with my fingers, with my own lips, until she stopped, but I managed to stay still, my hand plunged into the pocket of my jeans. If I'd moved, I couldn't guarantee I wouldn't touch her. After all, I was just a guy!

"You must think I'm, like, a total whacko," she said. "I don't know what to say now."

I concentrated on that damned lower lip.

"Um . . . So if you think that, I totally get it if you leave me now." She couldn't hold my gaze.

"No," I reassured her.

"No, what?"

"No, I don't think you're a whacko. Not at all." I took a step closer. Only a few inches separated us, and she leaned slightly back. "I'll stay," I said softly.

"OK." She swallowed hard.

"Let's find seats," I suggested.

We didn't speak during most of the trip. I didn't ask what had happened on the bus or why I would think she was nuts, though I was tempted several times. I didn't want to provoke another episode. Her behavior often surprised me, but I assumed she had her reasons.

When we finally spoke, she told me she was from Graz, where she had also gone to school and worked in the press office of a newspaper until a year ago.

"I like getting to know something about your life," I said.

"Well, I'm not such an open book, like you." She almost sounded defensive again.

"I guess that's right. I couldn't even find you on any social media." Almost everybody had an account somewhere these days.

"Oh, so you searched my name? And what did you find?" Mia folded her hands and looked at me.

"Nothing. Nothing at all. You sure are a riddle wrapped in a mystery. But I'll find out more about you. Trust me." I winked at her.

"Not everyone likes to lead such a public life, like you," she said. Then she fell silent again and stared out the window for a long time, her chin resting on her palm. She didn't again acknowledge my presence until shortly before we arrived in Rome.

She looked at me, biting her nails, then hastily hid her hands under her thighs. "The past several hours with you were really nice." She was once again chewing her lip, looking at the ground. "Thank you for helping me with my luggage."

"Mia . . ."

She raised her head.

"Let's keep traveling together." I didn't want her to journey alone. I wanted to learn more about her. There was something about her that was irresistible; it wasn't only her mannerisms I found captivating.

"I—I'm not sure," she stammered.

"What do you have to lose? I'm good company." I smiled at her.

"But—"

"But *whatever* is not an option. I want to show you Rome, off the beaten track," I said.

She lifted her hand as if to run her fingers through her hair, but then must have realized she was wearing that gray hat.

She exhaled. "OK."

"OK as in yes?" I asked and smiled.

"Yes. As in yes." She grinned.

"You won't regret it."

An announcement informed us we'd arrived.

"We should set up something for tomorrow morning. Where are you staying?"

"Um . . . it's called Cosmic Hotel, downtown."

"I'll come with you."

She stared at me with wide eyes.

"Don't worry. I'll have my own room," I reassured her. "It'll just be easier that way."

She nodded.

A cab dropped us off at the youth hostel, where they gave us adjacent rooms.

Mia stood at her door, grabbed the doorknob, and, hesitating, shifted her weight from one leg to the other.

"Have a good night, Samuel," she finally whispered.

God, I wanted to hug her. Hold her. Feel her head on my shoulder and inhale her vanilla scent. Support her. Never let her go again. Kiss the nape of her neck.

Instead, I only whispered back, "Good night, sweetie. Sleep well. I'll see you in the morning." Then I walked into my room.

Chapter 28
Mia—Let Me Show You More

Rome, June 2012

I tried to sleep, but I was too excited. What would the next day bring? Without Samuel, I would have more time for myself. More time to think about my comeback. But did I really want that?

No, I didn't. Samuel helped me forget. The only time I'd thought about my ordeal was when he'd asked why he couldn't find me online. I considered telling him why I had disappeared from the public world, but I didn't want the past to overshadow our encounter.

Before I fell asleep, I took out my sketchbook and pencils and began drawing like a madwoman. Illustrations would provide a record of my travels. Should my mother find them one day, she would know I'd been happy.

Around eight, just as I was getting out of the shower, I heard a knock coming from the hallway. I had only a towel wrapped around myself, and water dripped from my hair into my eyes and onto the tiles. Then came the unmistakable sound of someone entering my room. I hastened to close the bathroom door but slipped, fell, and landed on my butt. Surprised and in pain, I yelped.

"Mia?" It was Samuel.

"Turn around right now!" I yelled.

He obeyed. "Is there something I can do?"

I got up, still holding the towel. My butt hurt. "No, stay where you are! I'm not decent."

Samuel laughed. "Well, that certainly won't discourage me."

"Don't you dare!" I shouted.

"Don't panic. I won't budge an inch until you tell me to."

"Thank you." While getting dressed, I asked, "What are you doing in my room, anyway?"

He almost turned around.

"Stop!"

Samuel massaged his neck. "Sorry, but it's strange talking to someone this way."

I quickly zipped my vintage pink dress. "OK, now you can turn around."

Slowly, he did, then let his gaze wander my body from head to toe. The intensity in his eyes made me feel warm everywhere. "Wow, you look amazing." His gaze lingered on the top of my head. "I could have never imagined how beautiful you look without your hat. Wow . . ." he repeated again and smiled.

I felt my scalp. Oh shit. Trying to cover the feathery strands of hair with my hands, I desperately looked around. I began to panic. Gulping in air, I asked, "Do you see my hat anywhere?"

He looked puzzled and shook his head.

He took a few cautious steps toward me. Skirting past him, I grabbed up and emptied out my backpack, scattering my clothes everywhere. Helplessly from where I knelt on the floor, I looked up at him before continuing my frenzied search.

Samuel moved closer and leaned in as if he intended to touch me. Then he stopped and let his arm drop to his side. "Why?" he asked quietly.

"Why what?"

"Why do you need it?" He squatted down in front of me. "I don't understand why you do. You look great. Much better than with that piece of cotton on your head." Samuel's eyes wandered over me again. "You're perfect just as you are." His smile tried to convince me.

"Wool."

"Wool?" he echoed.

"The hat. It's wool, not cotton," I said.

"Fine. Forget about the *wool* hat." Softly, he added, "Believe me, you look awesome."

Heat rushed to my face. I didn't know where to look. My family was always telling me that I was still pretty, but I didn't believe them. They were my *family*—they were supposed to say things like that. Their words didn't help anyway, because every time I looked in the mirror, my reflection proved them wrong.

Nobody could seriously think of me as attractive.

Samuel noticed my doubt. "Believe me," he whispered. "Listen, I have a plan. If we find the hat, you put it back on and nobody but me will know how beautiful you are. I don't mind. But if you don't find it, you'll have to leave the room without it."

I agreed. What could I do? I didn't want to lock myself in here. But I had no idea where I had put it. Finally, admitting defeat, I walked out onto the street without it, trailing slowly after Samuel.

"Mia, if you don't speed up, I'll have to carry you." He laughed. "There's so much to see. Come on!"

Samuel was obviously excited to show me around Rome. Without him, I would have followed the tourist-beaten paths listed in the travel guides.

"I'm going to take you to one of the most beautiful places here."

Before he did, though, we had breakfast. Afterward, we walked for about thirty minutes until we reached the entrance to a park.

He swept his arm toward the entrance. "These are the Villa Borghese gardens. An emerald oasis."

I'd heard of this place, but without his encouragement, I would have probably skipped it. Once I was only a few yards in, though, I was thrilled we'd come. Everything was green, the greenest of greens. The paths were tidy. It was amazing.

"There's an art gallery in the middle of the park. Do you want to see it?"

I shook my head. "I want to stay right here."

He grinned. "We'll come back. Let's walk a little bit farther before that."

Chapter 29
Mia—My Body Says No

Rome, June 2012

Samuel led me to a pond with a small, Greek-inspired temple in the middle.

We lowered ourselves to the ground, close to the water. I smiled at Samuel. "Thank you."

"For what?"

"For all this." I gestured around with both arms. "And for being here." I looked into his gray eyes sparkling in the sunshine.

"My pleasure," he said, moving closer.

This time, exerting control over my usual reactions, I didn't flinch. I wanted him near me. Samuel stirred something inside that had been suppressed for a very long time. A desire to feel. To feel myself, and to feel others. Carefully, I edged toward him until only a foot remained between us. He looked into my eyes and crept even closer. With the closing of each inch, my heart beat quickened and the knot in my stomach tightened.

Samuel's gaze was intense. I was hardly aware of what was happening. My thoughts grew chaotic. A part of me wanted him to touch me, but everything else in me rejected that impulse, blocked it: Fear. My lack of self-confidence. The thought that the time I had left was too short. My anxieties increased, finally gaining the upper hand. Nervously, I circled my hand around my left arm. I could feel the scar through the fabric of my dress. I began scratching. My emotions were in turmoil, screaming that I must defy the feelings he was stirring to life. My whole already-unbalanced world was about to collapse. Everything would be consumed by confusion.

That must not happen.

I abruptly turned away and stared at the green water softly lapping at the shore. Samuel sighed, but he didn't say anything. I tucked up my legs, wrapping my arms around them so I could rest my chin on my knees.

We sat in silence for a long while, and I stared at the Temple of Aesculapius. A few tourists in rowboats passed by. In the shallow water close to the bank, countless doves bathed, dipping their beaks into the pond and shaking out their feathers to dry. Ducks quacked and chased each other across the surface. Yet it was still quiet enough that I could hear every movement Samuel made and every breath he took. Something deep inside me wanted to turn toward him. Wanted to look into those eyes again and feel his nearness. But my body said no. My body won. I wasn't ready yet.

"I don't want to cross your boundaries, Mia," Samuel eventually said.

I didn't look at him.

"It won't happen again. I simply got carried away."

"Don't worry. It . . . I probably sent out the wrong signals," I stammered. The vibe between us had turned awkward.

"No, no, really . . . I'll be more thoughtful next time."

I turned my head. Sam was watching me with sad, puppy-dog eyes. He was still sitting in the same position he'd first taken, legs slightly bent, ankles crossed, leaning slightly back on his propped-up arms. The snug fit of his faded black T-shirt with its Pac-Man logo accentuated the shape of his muscles, revealing how well built he was. I couldn't divert my eyes from his chest, fantasizing how it might feel to touch him there. Wondering if he'd shiver if I did. I tried to shake off my thoughts, literally by shaking my head, and then looked at him again. I could tell by the grin on his face that he'd noticed I'd been undressing him with my eyes. Blushing, I grinned.

"Let's go" was all I could say. I got up and, after a few steps, realized he wasn't behind me. I looked around. He was still sitting on the grass, staring at me, a broad smile on his face. With a gesture of my head, I motioned him to join me.

He jumped to his feet and said, "OK, OK. I'm coming."

Chapter 30
Samuel—More Rome

Rome, June 2012

I mean, go figure, right? It was obvious Mia was attracted to me. How would I not have sensed it in that moment at the pond? Mia was hot, period. A guy just had to look at her to get, well, turned on. And now that she wasn't wearing that gray scrap of cloth anymore, she was even hotter. I wouldn't tell her that I had found her hat under her bed. She didn't need it. Nothing about her needed hiding. I wasn't lying when I'd told her she looked amazing. She did. And much more. She radiated something special, something enigmatic, but she concealed it well. Maybe she wasn't even aware of her uniqueness. But if she was, she seemed to be trying everything in her power to suppress it, and she was damned good at doing so. Everything about her shouted "Leave me alone!" But her tough facade was beginning to crumble.

I could tell, by comparing the way she acted now with how she'd behaved when we'd met on the train. Now she wanted more. Mia wanted to touch and she wanted to feel. I'd pretended to be asleep on the bus when she'd caressed my face. I had kept as still as I could, otherwise I knew she would have flinched away. I'd enjoyed her touch, so gentle, almost imperceptible. When she'd caressed my lips, I'd wanted to open my eyes and take her sweet face between my hands. Instead of her fingertips, I wanted to feel her full red lips on mine. When she'd withdrawn her fingers, I'd startled some. Her warmth was gone. Guess I wanted more, too.

When we were at the pond, I nearly threw myself at her. I'd promised myself that I'd leave her alone, that I wouldn't touch her. That I wouldn't look at her as if I wanted to undress her. But hell, she made it very difficult. I only needed to see those shimmering eyes for a moment, and I was totally lost. My body reacted with an independence all its own.

I moved in again. The breeze swept her sweet vanilla aroma into the air. I shifted closer still and looked into her eyes. For a long time, she held my gaze. Then she abruptly turned away. I could have guessed that would happen.

She acted as if nothing had occurred between us and, after a few minutes, was back to wearing her usual mask, smiling as if everything was normal. Maybe she really didn't like me, didn't want me. Maybe I had totally misread her. But, really, hadn't *she* undressed *me* with her eyes, too?

She got up. "Let's go," was all she said. She walked a few steps. I continued sitting, hypnotized by her beauty, then she turned and motioned for me to join her.

I grinned and said, "OK, OK. I'm coming."

As we strolled along, I asked, "Where do you want to go next?"

She smiled. "I've always wanted to see St. Peter's."

"Your wish is my command." I winked at her.

We continued walking, then Mia abruptly stopped and turned to me. "I've assumed you know your way around in Rome. At least that's what you've led me to believe."

"That's right," I said.

Mia crossed her arms over her chest. "Then why are we walking in the wrong direction?"

"Are we?" I raised my eyebrows and scratched my head.

"I'm not particularly great with directions, maps, or the like, but I'm pretty sure St. Peter's is not far from the hostel. This part of town looks totally unfamiliar."

"Don't worry, sweetie. I promised to show you St. Peter's, and I will. Just from another angle. And without standing in line. Well, not as long of a line."

She bit her lip again, and I looked away from the temptation she presented.

"OK, then. I guess I'll keep following you."

"You'll be glad—I'm sure of it." I smiled.

We walked up the Aventine Hill until we reached the monastery of the Knights of Malta.

"A high wall?" she asked.

"Oh yes." I grinned.

"It's really beautiful here, looks like a very nice residential neighborhood. But what's here to show me?"

"Come a little closer. Fortunately, nobody else is here right now," I said and, without thinking twice, reached out my hand. Oops, damn it . . .

But Mia didn't flinch. Instead, she inspected my hand and seemed to think about actually taking it. But she only raised her head and smiled at me. "Well then, show me what you want to show me." She didn't grab my hand.

"See the big gate?" We approached a large, iron entrance. "Just peep through the keyhole."

Mia looked at me, confused. "And why would I do that?"

"You really haven't researched your trip very well," I said.

"I didn't research anything. I didn't really have a plan of where I wanted to go. I'm playing it by ear," she said, this time more seriously.

"Great. So we can continue being spontaneous together."

"With pleasure." She was smiling again. Why didn't she wear that smile all the time?

"Now look through the keyhole."

She leaned forward. "St. Peter's," she whispered.

"See? I told you!" My surprise was a success.

Chapter 31
Mia—My Rules

Rome and beyond, June 2012

I had been traveling with Samuel for almost a week now and enjoying every minute of it. He made me laugh. He knew when it was best to be silent. The most important thing was he respected that I didn't want any intimacy. Well, I did want intimacy, but I couldn't handle it. In any case, Samuel didn't try to touch me again. I wasn't sure whether I liked that or not.

We spent three days in Rome. After our first unconventional day, I insisted on seeing the typical sites—Colosseum, Castel Sant'Angelo, Sistine Chapel, and St. Peter's Basilica. This time, up close. As he'd predicted, we had to wait far too long in lines. But the time sped by with Sam by my side.

Over lunch one day, I gathered all my courage.

"Um . . . Samuel?"

He looked up from his plate and motioned at mine. "What's the matter? Don't you like the food?"

I shook my head. "That's not it."

"Then why aren't you eating? You do know that coffee in the morning doesn't count as a meal, right?" He looked worried. "When *do* you eat, anyway? I've only seen you nibble on some white bread, and that was yesterday."

I frowned. I really didn't feel like discussing my dietary choices. "I eat when I'm hungry." I'd heard this lecture often enough from my family. "And I'll eat more later."

"Good. Otherwise, I might just force-feed you." He grinned. "Anyway, what were you saying?"

I ran my fingers through my short hair. I still hadn't found my hat. Kriszta had done a good job as a hair stylist, but right now, I wished I'd brought two hats.

I rested my hands in my lap and began picking a cuticle. "I only wanted . . . um . . ." I couldn't find the right words. I'd never stammered like this before my illness. I looked into Samuel's eyes and started over. "I'm not sure where you're headed after Rome, but it'd be nice if we could continue traveling together. At least for a little while longer."

"I thought that was a given," he said matter-of-factly and continued eating.

That evening, we sat in my room and planned our itinerary. We couldn't just roam aimlessly all the time. We decided our next stop would be Nice, where we figured there'd be plenty of sights to see.

When we arrived in Nice, the city's charm almost overwhelmed me. I didn't want to schedule anything; I only wanted to explore the narrow streets and back alleys. Stroll the outdoor markets. Savor each moment.

Noticing how happy just meandering wherever I felt like made me, Samuel agreed to anything I suggested.

Grinning at me, he said, "Let's spend a few days here."

I flashed him a genuine smile. This city felt so vibrant. And suddenly there it was again, finally—a long-missed, incredibly amazing happiness inside me.

There was only one problem. Samuel said he'd had enough of cheap beds. I bit my tongue and didn't point out that he'd slept in a *cheap bed* for only three days, which wasn't that long. He insisted we stay in a hotel. And not just any hotel. No, he wanted one of the most expensive ones, one way outside my budget. I decided to leave to find a hostel, but he didn't want me spending the night by myself in a foreign city. That was very sweet of him, but what choice did I have?

We went back and forth for a long time before he finally convinced me to go with him to a hotel he chose, saying he'd pay. I accepted on the condition that it would be for only one night, and that I would have my own room, preferably the smallest one available.

"OK, you got it. After that, we can go back to those fleabags again. That is, if you don't notice how amazing the mattresses are here," he added with a wink as we entered the lobby.

"You wait and see. I won't stay more than one night. Believe me, I've slept in far worse than youth hostels." For instance, in the hospital during my prolonged stays, week after week, on a hard bed, and while lying perfectly still. I closed my eyes and raised a hand to massage my temple. I didn't want to think about this right now.

"We have only one room left," the man at the front desk said.

"We'll take it," Samuel answered.

I stared at him. The clerk began typing something into the computer. "You can't do this," I hissed.

He looked at me with innocent eyes. "Why not? We won't be there much anyway. And I'm actually saving money."

I continued to glare at him. "It was your idea to spend the night here. You offered to pay for my room. I didn't want it. And now you're whining about money? As if you don't have a shitload of it?"

The man at the front desk looked up briefly, then continued typing.

Samuel stared me down. "Forget about the money. It's not about the money. Besides I could pay for as many nights as we want. The bottom line is I won't leave you alone. And I don't want to go back to a hostel with backbreaking beds. Please, let's take this room," he implored.

I crossed my arms over my chest. "All right. But there will be rules."

He laughed.

We filled out the required documents, and the clerk handed us the key.

In the room, I plopped down on the oversized canopy bed and let myself fall back. The mattress was perfectly soft. The sheets smelled marvelous. This was awesome . . .

With a broad grin, Samuel walked past me and tossed his backpack on the sofa. "I see you're already enjoying yourself."

I straightened up quickly. "It's just a bed." A very comfortable bed, but I would never admit that.

"I'll ask you again tomorrow if you still feel it's *just a bed*."

I rolled my eyes. "Let me tell you my rules now," I said. Sam took a seat at the foot of the huge mattress. I scooted to the middle and sat cross-legged, facing him. "Number one. This is *my* bed."

Samuel burst into gales of laughter. I crossed my arms and waited for him to quiet. He finally wiped at the tears in his eyes but continued to chuckle. "You said the sofa would be fine."

"I've changed my mind," I said. "I've been sitting on this bed for only five minutes, and I don't intend to abandon it."

"Ha! I knew it," he exclaimed. "But you can have it."

"Thank you," I said.

I continued, "The bathroom is off-limits whenever I'm in there. Even if I'm only brushing my teeth or my hair."

He nodded.

"Not even a peek is permitted, at all, when I'm in my pajamas and especially not when I'm getting dressed."

"That's it?"
Now I nodded.
"I think I can manage," he said.

Chapter 32
Samuel—Close to You

Nice, June 2012

We didn't leave the hotel room that night. The long train rides had exhausted Mia. It was obvious she needed sleep, which was a big reason why I'd wanted to treat her to a stay at a good hotel. I also would not spend another night in a youth hostel. Maybe I was spoiled, but I'd had my fill of bad mattresses.

Although this night wouldn't be much better, since I'd agreed to let Mia have the bed. Then again, I wanted to give her something nice, so I wouldn't mind—too much—another uncomfortable night.

Abiding by her other rules, too, I also didn't glance her direction when she was in her pajamas, not even when she crossed the room after she'd emerged from changing in the bathroom. That doesn't mean I wouldn't have liked to steal a peek, but I was allowed to turn around only after she'd pulled the duvet on the bed up to her chin. That's how she wanted things, and I respected her wishes. I was, of course, very aware by then that she shied away from anything to do with intimacy.

We ordered room service, talked for a while, then turned on the TV. Mia moved to one side of the bed and motioned for me to use the other so I could see the screen better. She didn't have to ask twice. I would have liked to edge even closer to her. Her vanilla scent was driving me crazy.

"Does your shower gel smell like vanilla?" I couldn't help asking.

She looked at me puzzled. "Why would you think that?"

I shook my head. "It's probably just whatever they use to wash the sheets." But I knew the sweet aroma was hers.

She looked at me skeptically. "Whatever you say. I don't smell anything."

She dropped off soon after that. I got up, grabbed the other duvet and a pillow, and walked over to the sofa. Almost as soon as I lay down, I was asleep, too.

My slumber didn't last long. A strident scream and bitter weeping woke me. Struggling up from sleep, I tried to remember where I was.

Then I heard it again. Mia was wailing in her sleep. She sounded so tortured. So frightened. Moonlight slid through the crack between the curtains and fell onto the bed, where I could see her thrashing about, her face contorted with pain. I bolted up, still half-asleep and hurried over to the bed.

"Hey, Mia! Wake up. It's just a dream. Sweetie, wake up." My words didn't seem to penetrate. I lowered myself to the bed. Damn it, what should I do? I didn't know what would happen if I touched her. Carefully, I rested my hand on her shoulder, hoping to calm her down. "Mia," I repeated. "Sweetie, it's only a dream."

Her scream again split the night. Shit!

"Mia, my sweetheart. It's me, Samuel. Shh. It's OK." I was so worried by now that I was having trouble staying calm myself. I slid down a little further beside her, continuing to lightly grasp her shoulder, then very gently, I stroked her cheeks. Finally, she relaxed. Her cries stopped and she lay quietly.

"Samuel, please stay," she whispered drowsily and snuggled up to my side.

I wasn't sure what to do. Did she really want me with her? Her rules had been more than clear, and she'd seemed intent on strictly enforcing them. When she'd been in the bathroom, she'd called several times to make sure I wasn't looking before she'd opened the door. Even when we'd sat next to each other on the train, she'd leaned against the window, as far from me as possible, obviously avoiding even the slightest touch.

And now this?

She nestled closer to me and murmured my name.

"Mia?" I whispered. No answer. She was sound asleep, her right arm slung around my chest and her left arm under her head.

I closed my eyes and focused on her warmth. The physical contact made my skin tingle in the most wonderful way. I didn't want to push her off. She must have said my name for a reason, even if she was dreaming.

I settled in more comfortably. Once I had found a restful position, I pulled up the duvet and held her tight. Mia sighed softly and burrowed in again. The arm around my chest moved. Slowly, her hand wandered across my skin until her palm finally came to rest over my heart.

I closed my eyes and inhaled deeply. Then I let all the air out through my nose, smelling the sweet vanilla that was her. She sighed, a contented sound. I didn't know what to think. Was she completely asleep? I was too comfortable, too happy like this to leave her bed. I liked the way her warm body nestled against me, the way her fingertips with their roughened nails had brushed my chest.

"Samuel?" She said my name again.

"I'm here," I whispered against her hair.

"Please, stay," she repeated.

"I will. Right next to you," I murmured and softly kissed her forehead.

Chapter 33
Mia—Dr. Weiß, Help Please!

Nice, June 2012

I woke up because I was hot, very hot. My arm had fallen asleep, and it prickled as if a thousand ants were crawling over it. Then I realized my hand was resting on something warm, something firm. Something emanating a lot of heat. Carefully, I moved my fingers. It was a body. A male body. My heart began to race, and I quickly looked over.

Samuel . . .

Startled, I scooted away from him. My entire body trembled . . . I desperately needed air. A huge lump stuck in my throat and blocked my windpipe. What was Samuel Winter doing in my bed?

My heart hammered so violently, it almost hurt. It felt as if it were about to explode.

Air . . .

Breathe . . .

I was panting as I slowly managed to get out of the bed. I needed air. A lot of it. Inhale. Exhale. I tried to relax my stiff fingers, without success.

I snatched up my phone from the bedside table. Away . . . I had to get away as fast as possible. Steadying myself by grasping on to pieces of furniture, I staggered into the bathroom.

I slammed the door behind me. My knees buckled, and I sank onto the cool tiles. My heart raced, and a whooshing in my ears grew louder and louder.

With what little strength remained, I tapped in Dr. Weiß's number. I put the phone on speaker and placed it on the floor next to me.

"Mia?" a drowsy voice asked.

"Dr. Weiß, I need your help." I could barely articulate the words. I needed more oxygen.

"How can I help you at this early hour?" His voice was calm.

"Air," I croaked.

Immediately, he realized what was happening. "Mia, listen to me. Do not think of the trigger. Simply concentrate on your breathing." His words were soothing. I heard him inhale deeply. "Now breathe with me. Close your eyes. Inhale. Exhale. Let all the air out of your lungs. Inhale . . ."

I focused on his words. I closed my eyes and did the best I could. It hurt.

"Exhale through your mouth."

Exhale . . .

"And repeat." His tone was both gentle and commanding. I summoned all my strength. "Do not forget to move." I moved my fingers. "I can hear you're breathing normally again. Great job. I'm proud of you, Mia," Dr. Weiß said. "Now tell me what happened. I know you can do it. There won't be another panic attack."

"Samuel happened," I blurted without providing further explanation.

"Well, if you let me know who Samuel is, I might be able to follow."

"He . . . I met him on the train. Somehow we've continued traveling together. I—I don't really know why. But I couldn't let him go." I began picking my cuticle until it hurt, tearing at the skin so fiercely that it bled.

"What is going on with Samuel?" he asked calmly.

"He's in my bed." I felt the panic creep up again. I began huffing.

"Concentrate on your breathing," Dr. Weiß said. "Now, Samuel. Who is he?"

I took another deep breath. "We met on the first day of my trip. Um . . . He—he was sneaking through my sketchbook. Well, not really sneaking. He said he was fascinated, so he looked at the drawings."

"I'm glad to hear you're making good use of your talent and your sketchbook. Go on." I heard the sound of a coffeemaker percolating in the background.

"I had a panic attack and almost passed out. I would never have fended it off by myself, but then I looked into his eyes." I paused for a moment, recalling their gray shimmer. "Then I felt better."

I heard Dr. Weiß sip his coffee. "You found a calm anchor." He sounded happy for me. "Why, then, are you panicking?"

"We parted ways at the station and then ran into each other two days later. By coincidence, we had the same destination. Then he helped me in a bad situation. "I ran my fingers through my hair and bit my lower lip. "He helped me get over yet another panic attack. But there's more," I whispered. "Dr. Weiß, I didn't want him to leave, so I asked him if we could travel on together. But I'm so worried he thinks I'm a whacko."

"Why would he think that?" he asked.

"You know how I am. The touching. Fear of everything new. I could go on. So you tell me how someone wouldn't think I'm crazy."

"You're not crazy, Mia. You've just been through a lot."

A hell of a lot, and that's why Samuel shouldn't have a place in my life. Not under these circumstances.

"You like him, don't you?" he said.

I really didn't want to think about what Samuel could mean to me. He didn't know me. I didn't know him, even if it felt as if I had known him forever. Which was exactly what scared me so much. I just didn't understand what this meant, any of it.

"I'm not sure, Dr. Weiß. He shouldn't be in my life."

"Maybe he should. Do you feel comfortable around him?"

I closed my eyes and leaned my head against the door. "I wish things were different," I said quietly.

"You should be grateful he's there. You feel calmed by his presence. You need him. Does he make you laugh?"

"Yes," I admitted, barely audible.

"Are you happy when you see him?"

"I can't imagine this trip without him." There. I'd said it out loud. I really couldn't. And I didn't want to. Although I knew I would break his heart.

"Then why are you so afraid?" he persisted.

"I don't know how he ended up in my bed. He had one arm wrapped around me, and my hand rested on his chest." The mere thought of it caused my heart to race. "The touch . . ."

"You're still struggling with it. But you don't need to. He isn't a stranger anymore. Stop thinking so much. Follow your heart," he said.

He had a point there. Samuel was not a stranger. He hadn't been a stranger, not from the moment we'd met.

"Talk to him and find out what happened."

"OK," I sighed softly.

"Live your life, Mia. *Live* it."

Then he hung up.

Chapter 34
Mia—My Crappy Life

Nice, June 2012

I stared at the display until it turned off. Now it was entirely dark in the bathroom. I grabbed my hair with both hands and pulled it fiercely.

Ahhhh . . . damn it, damn it, damn it . . .

I didn't know what to do. Was I ready to follow my heart? Could I make it? What would happen when the shit really hit the fan? Would I ruin Samuel?

He banged on the door. The banging grew more incessant . . .

"Mia, please open the door. Please," Samuel begged.

I closed my eyes. My head was about to explode any minute. My emotions were about to rip me apart from the inside. Samuel was special. He didn't think of me as sick. Didn't comment on my behavior. But he was doomed.

"Mia, please," he pleaded.

Carefully, I stood up, fumbled for the light, and walked over to the sink. I looked in the mirror and rubbed my face. I wiped the tears from my cheeks, took a deep breath, and opened the door. Samuel's arm was raised to bang again, but he lowered it. My eyes wandered over his torso. He looked even better than I had imagined. This barely dressed perfect body certainly didn't make things easier.

"I am so sorry, Mia. I can explain everything." He nodded toward the bathroom. "May I come in?"

I nodded, but couldn't avoid biting my lip.

"And would you please stop doing this?"

I frowned.

"I mean, I'm only a man, after all."

I forced myself to stop, but it is not easy to change lifelong habits. I began tapping with my feet. I had to do something.

"You must have had a bad dream," he began. "I tried to wake you up, but it didn't work." He took one step forward, and I took one step back. "You murmured you wanted me to stay. I . . . I wasn't sure if that was the right thing to do." He ran his fingers through his hair and folded his hands behind his neck. "But you repeated it and just snuggled up by my side."

My eyes grew wide. "Never," I said.

Samuel nodded. "Oh yes you did. Otherwise I wouldn't have stayed with you. You were so peaceful, so—"

"OK, OK, I got it," I interrupted and massaged my temples. My subconscious did exactly what Dr. Weiß wanted me to do.

"Mia, seriously. I—"

I cut him off again, gesturing with one raised hand. "Don't." I walked past him and sat down on the bed.

He followed me. "What was going on in there?"

I inhaled deeply and shook my head. "Believe me, you don't want to know."

Sam squatted in front of me. "What if I do want to know?" he asked quietly. "Look, Mia, I'm not blind. I can tell you want more." Frustrated, he stood again. "Damn it . . ." He punched a fist against the wall. "Why am I not allowed to touch you? I can feel the chemistry. What is your goddamn problem?" he shouted. "Why am I not even allowed to hold your hand?" He paced the room.

I just stared at him. I had not expected that. I had no clue he was feeling that way. He had always been so thoughtful, and had never even attempted to make a pass. Nothing. I needed a few minutes to gather my thoughts.

"You are not allowed," I finally said, "because I am not allowed. Do you understand? You do not want to get involved in my crappy life. I hate myself. I can't even look at myself." I jumped to my feet, rushed to my backpack and frenetically began packing. Samuel didn't say a word. He just stood there, petrified and stared at the floor.

I pointed at my body. "Look at me." He didn't move. "Look at me, for heaven's sake." My voice rose so loud it cracked. I was livid. I was angry at myself, at everything, at . . . I didn't really know why exactly.

He looked at me. "I can't wrap my head around you. Mia, just look at yourself. You are just . . . amazing. Don't you notice how everyone looks at you? Do you have any idea why?"

"I know quite well why everyone's gawking at me," I screamed. "I hate it when they do that. Not even here I'm safe."

Another puzzled look. "What the heck are you talking about?"

"I'm sure that's why I attracted your attention, right?" I pulled my hair violently. "That's why. Everyone can see I'm sick. It's obvious. I can't hide it."

Samuel looked very confused. Cautiously, he came a few steps closer. "You don't look sick, sweetie. You look magnificent. Even in these pink pajamas. I just, like you, Mia." He smiled.

I gave him a sad look. "Samuel, you can cut it out now." I slumped to the floor. "You can stop pretending."

He shook his head. "I still don't get it."

My voice was very quiet and monotonous. "Samuel, I *am* sick. Was sick . . . Whatever. My body reveals it all."

Again he shook his head.

"Do you remember when we first met? I remember it very well, because I was about to have a panic attack. I hate it when strangers touch me." I took a deep breath. The lump in my throat was back. "You must have been taken aback by my crazy behavior. This damned breathing technique is pretty obvious."

"Mia . . ." He touched his hair. "A panic attack?" Poor, confused Samuel.

"Your fingers touched me. You are a stranger. That's what happens."

Samuel came closer. "But I'm not a stranger anymore." I looked at the carpet. "Please, look at me." I inhaled deeply. Our eyes met. "I'm no longer a stranger." He reached out his hand and waited. "I'm already part of your life." He was a part of my life, no matter if he disappeared now or stayed. We would never be able to erase this memory.

My heart was racing. With a trembling hand I reached out until only a few millimeters were left between Samuel's fingertips and mine.

He smiled. "Breathe." I already knew how it felt to touch his skin, but this was different. Samuel was awake now and could do more than I was ready for. All I wanted was some closeness, to feel his warmth.

"You tell me when it's enough and I'll stop," he promised. "Just say the word." I nodded and carefully put my hand into his palm. He smiled at me. I took his other hand. My heart raced, but this time, it was because I was so excited, and happiness pulsed through my veins. I moved closer to him. Our knees almost touched. I put my left hand over his heart. It was pounding fast. Samuel was just as excited as I was. He raised his other hand, but paused before touching my cheek. With his eyes, he asked me whether it was OK. I nodded.

Very tenderly, he caressed my skin. I felt goose bumps all over my body. I had forgotten these feelings. I was so glad I finally allowed them.

Chapter 35
Samuel—The Truth

Nice, June 2012

Mia and I sat there for what felt like forever, with my hand on her cheek and her hand over my heart. We didn't speak. It was peaceful, blissful. I just can't describe it. I'd never experienced anything as intimate as this moment.

"Come," I said to her finally, and she followed me to the bed. We sat down, leaning against each other, still holding hands.

"What happened?" I asked carefully. She looked at me with tears in her eyes. "You don't need to tell me if you don't want to," I assured her.

She seemed to consider how much to reveal and began biting her lip again. I reached out, and she flinched.

"I won't hurt you," I said softly. With my thumb, I gently stroked her lower lip, rescuing it from her teeth. Her lip was incredibly soft. One spot was a little chapped, and I longed to soothe it with a tender kiss. Slowly, I lowered my hand. Mia closed her eyes and inhaled deeply. Then she opened them. They glistened.

"Everything happened way too fast. If I hadn't been so sick, who knows where I'd be now?" She looked at our joined hands. "Samuel, I really wanted to end it all." Mia rolled up her left sleeve, uncovering a pale pink scar across her entire lower arm. There were smaller, faded pockmarks from stitches along either side. She stared at the old injury she'd done herself, lost in her thoughts. I didn't know what to say or if I should say anything at all.

Then she continued, "Please don't judge me."

"I would never do that." She must have had her reasons.

"For a long time, I thought it would've been better had I never learned the truth. Then, one day, I would have just been gone. Not knowing would have spared me a lot." At first, I didn't get what she saying.

"Do you know what it's like to want to die?" She closed her eyes and breathed hard through her nose. "No, how could you?" She shook her head. Worried she might stop talking if I said even one word, I kept quiet.

"I was in constant pain. One day I was healthy; the next day I was sick."

Mia took a deep breath. *"From now on, every new day is a day you need to win. Day after day. This is not about long-term goals anymore. Those sentences still echo in my mind."* She dug her fingernails into my flesh.

"The prognosis was poor. How can anyone deal with that? Boom. Over. Forget about a carefree life. But how can you go on when you don't want to continue, not like that?" Her tears ran freely. She struggled to compose herself. "Dr. Weiß showed me that life can go on, somehow. I stuck around for my family's sake. Because I didn't want to cause them even more pain."

I was still at a loss. I only understood she wasn't well. Finally, she looked at me. Our eyes locked. "Diagnosis: skin cancer," she whispered.

Those words cut right through my heart. It wasn't long ago that I'd learned someone else I knew had experienced the same disease. In that case, the news had reached me too late. But why Mia? She was so young.

She looked at the floor and murmured, "The whole nine yards. Surgery, chemotherapy. And sure enough, I suffered every possible side effect." She looked at me again. "I didn't want to go on like that, Samuel. I couldn't see any sense in why I'd contracted cancer. They say everything happens for a reason. What's the reason? Where's the sense in getting so sick? You tell me."

"We wouldn't have met if you hadn't," I offered.

A faint smile touched her lips. "That's true. But I wouldn't have fallen into such a deep hole, either. I've been battling for over a year now. To get my life back on track. I've only made baby steps, though. I'm still afraid of too many situations. Afraid of touching, of remembering . . . and then there are the dreams. I never recall them, but I feel miserable when I wake up."

"Look, you're making progress. You're holding my hand. Moving forward is what counts." She nodded. Tears were still rolling down her cheeks. "Are you healed?" I asked.

She looked up at the ceiling, and I could see her struggle to stop crying. Chewing her lip again, she returned her gaze to my face and nodded. I squeezed her hand. She smiled a little.

Dawn broke through the window. The weather would be beautiful today, ideal for a stroll through the old town. Or the beach. But we didn't feel up to it. We spent the rest of the day in the room. Ordered food and watched TV.

Then Mia opened up, and more details of her life poured out. It made me happy that she felt comfortable enough now to confide in me. I didn't want to pity her, because I knew she hated that. But I couldn't help it. I wanted to hug her and never let her go. She desperately needed tenderness, but she would have pushed me away. She didn't want to feel pressured.

I listened for a long time. Mia didn't seem to expect any responses from me. I couldn't understand how people had turned their backs on her. Like her boyfriend, who had been so cold and selfish, conducting an affair when she'd needed him most. I was furious for her and thought that guy better hope he never crossed my path.

It pained me to see her like this, bouncing from one mood to the next. One moment, she laughed; the next moment, she was gloomy. She paused often to compose herself. Then she would look at me and continue. She didn't let go of my hand for most of the day and even moved so we sat closer together.

It was evening when she finally leaned her head against my shoulder. "Thank you for listening."

"My pleasure," I murmured against her hair, inhaling her sweet aroma.

"You know," Mia started and looked at me, "you're the first person I've told everything to. The others know only bits and pieces about what's going on, been going on, with me. Not even my therapist has heard the whole story. If he knew I'd confided in someone I've known for only a few days . . ."

I placed a soft kiss on her hair. "Thank you for sharing."

She smiled at me. "I feel good around you."

Chapter 36
Mia—Happy Tears

Nice, June 2012

I finally followed my heart. Maybe I should have done so earlier. Maybe it would have kept me from careening into that deep, dark hole. Then again, there wasn't anywhere my heart would have wanted to go. Until now.

We didn't speak about my illness anymore. I didn't want to. I had told him everything. Well, almost everything. I had spared him the details. Or maybe I had spared myself.

In any case, I was glad Samuel didn't press me to elaborate, although I could tell he was thinking about it. He seemed lost in his thoughts. Especially at night, when we were back in the room. I watched him play his guitar as he stared out the window. I could see he was somewhere else while he plucked random melodies and quietly sang along. In those moments, it was obvious he didn't want to talk. I didn't mind. I enjoyed just listening to his voice, studying his features. He became my favorite subject, and soon I'd filled page after page of my sketchbook with his image. I had missed drawing. I'd missed the smudged fingers and the sound of the pencil scratching on the paper.

I didn't understand what was happening inside me. Was I on my way back? Feelings I had thought long dead were returning, joined by new and unfamiliar emotions.

Maybe they rose out of the resumption of tactile sensations. Physical touch made me nervous, but in a good way now. I allowed Samuel to hold my hand as much as he wanted. As much as I wanted. Each time he did, pure happiness rushed through my body.

Samuel no longer had to sleep on the sofa; I promoted him to a place beside me on the comfy bed.

"I thought you wanted to return to one of your awesome hostels." He laughed.

"OK, OK. You won. I won't insist any longer."

"Ha! I knew it." He grinned. Crossing my arms over my chest, I pretended to be angry and he raised his hands apologetically.

"I already admitted you won, so there's no need for a victory dance. But I have one condition—I'll pay you back every single cent."

"We'll see about that." He winked.

"Samuel!" I snapped. All he did was continue smiling.

We stayed four days in Nice. After we had spent the first in our room, we filled the remaining time with strolls through the city and along the beach. It was a leisurely pace, enjoyable after rushing from one site to the next in Rome. The last day in Nice was particularly special.

As we walked through the old, narrow streets, I let my fingers trail over the sandstone walls. Despite the sunshine, the surfaces were cool. All my senses were awakened. I drew in a great breath, closed my eyes, and continued on. Unseeing, I couldn't avoid bumping into Samuel's side.

"What are you doing?" he asked.

I peeked up and smiled at him. "I am enjoying." We paused. "Just close your eyes and listen. Breathe. Concentrate on the sounds and smells around you. Then tell me about them."

He grabbed my hand, closed his eyes, and took a gulp of air. "I smell warmth. And I hear cars, many cars," he said.

"Listen more closely."

He inhaled again and was quiet for a moment. "I hear the sea. Birds. Laughter." He intertwined his fingers with mine and stepped closer. "I can hear a rhythm that is strong and steady."

I moved toward him, too, and closed my eyes.

"I smell the sun and the pines," I whispered. We stood very close now. "I hear a rhythm that is strong and steady, too."

"I smell vanilla," he murmured. My heart was racing as I took one final step, closing the space between us, and pressed my body against his. I felt his heart beat, and then I felt mine, pounding faster and faster. His warmth pulsed through my veins. It was almost too much.

"Breathe, sweetie. Don't forget to breathe," Samuel said. I gasped for air. "And exhale."

I let out the air from my lungs.

"We can stop if you want to."

I felt his warm breath on my face. I could only nod.

"I hope that was a yes. My eyes are still closed. Should I open them?"

"No. No, keep them shut," I said quickly.

"OK . . ." He lowered his head. I felt the tip of his nose on mine. "Breathe."

I stood on tiptoe and put his hands around my back. I inhaled again and, trembling, wrapped my arms around his neck. I stretched my own to tilt up my face. When our lips touched, the kiss felt as soft as the touch of a feather. "Don't go further," I whispered against his mouth. We stood very still and enjoyed the moment. The moment I had been able to let Samuel come as close as he was. It felt wonderful. I felt tears slowly trace their way down my cheeks and moisten our lips.

"Don't cry, Mia."

I swallowed hard.

"Open your eyes." His voice was soft yet determined. My heart was still pounding. I obeyed. My tears were now streaming, and he wiped them away with his thumbs. "Did I do something wrong?"

"No, not at all. It just feels . . . overwhelming," I sobbed.

"Then why this waterfall?" He smiled.

"I like it." I paused. "I like this feeling." I answered his smile.

Samuel cupped my face in his hands. "I like this feeling, too," he whispered and kissed my forehead.

Chapter 37
Mia—Music for Life

En route to Marseille, July 2012

Traveling with Samuel was so much more fun than traveling alone. I even had my own personal jukebox during the long train rides—although I wasn't the only one enjoying Samuel's music, as evidenced by the giggling girls across the aisle.

"How often does this happen to you?" Actually, I could understand their reaction quite well. There was no way of *not* admiring Samuel. Even I hadn't been able to ignore him, despite my best efforts. Those beautiful eyes had instantly captured me.

"What do you mean?" He frowned.

"Those giggling young things would just love your company." My gaze indicated them. Sam turned around.

"Somebody will notice," I whispered, embarrassed.

Samuel smiled at the two, then winked. "Oh, come on, Mia. Let me have some fun." His grin broadened, and the two girls' nervous laughter grew. I wished I hadn't said anything because soon I could feel their gazes move on to me, sizing me up.

Samuel stopped playing. "Sweetie, you OK? You look very pale all of a sudden." He took my hand.

"I shouldn't have said anything," I blurted. "Look how they're staring at me now." I tried to hide my face behind my hand, but Samuel reached out and grabbed it. I looked at the floor.

"There is absolutely no reason you should hide from anyone. Believe me. Let them stare. They're probably wondering what a beautiful woman like you is doing with an ordinary guy like me."

I raised my eyes to his. I wasn't buying his words, but it was sweet of him to try to lift my spirits. "Thank you."

"I mean it," he insisted. Slowly, he leaned forward. I didn't move. By now, having him this close caused merely a slight nervousness, which was good. I enjoyed the tingling and prickling sensations that came with it. He came nearer, and his soft lips touched my forehead as lightly as a gentle breeze. I inhaled deeply and closed my eyes, surrounded by the scent of his piney cologne. His lips still touching my forehead, he murmured, "You are the most beautiful woman I have ever met. I fell for you the moment I saw you." I didn't know what to say. I could concentrate only on the heat I felt rushing into my cheeks. Samuel leaned back and smiled at me.

"Play another song," I said, and he resumed plucking at the strings.

After some time had passed, he asked, "Why do you need music, even while you sleep?"

Nobody had ever asked me that. Or maybe nobody had noticed. It was true, though. I wore my earbuds almost all of the time, even at home.

"Um . . . I guess I just like it," I said.

He shook his head. "No, there must be more to it. You used to play an instrument, didn't you? When you don't have your earbuds in, you're either humming or singing under your breath."

Was I really?

"It sounds great," he assured me.

I looked down at my fingers and began to pick a cuticle. "It's the only thing left that reminds me there's still life to be lived." I searched out his gray eyes with my own. "Music helps me to better deal with my emotions. I couldn't play anymore, so listening gives me something to fill that void. It helps me to feel myself."

"I hear you." He averted his gaze, apparently lost in thought for a moment, then returned to studying me. "You stopped playing the instrument because of your illness?"

I nodded.

"But why? When it is so important to you?"

Apparently this was some sort of Q&A session. I was glad the ride to Marseille wouldn't take long. "I was too tired. My fingers were too stiff, which doesn't make them much good for playing the piano," I explained, then changed the topic. "Enough questions for today. Once we get to Marseille, let's find a Laundromat. All my clothes are dirty."

"Well, you'll just have to walk around naked," he whispered and brushed my cheek with the back of his hand.

I felt excitement rush through my veins and a fluttering set up in my stomach. "Yeah, I can see you would like that." I grinned.

Samuel nodded, beaming.

"Guys . . ." I groaned, rolling my eyes and sitting back. I wanted a quick snooze before we arrived in Marseille. As sleep descended, I realized happiness had seeped into every cell of my body.

"We're almost there," he whispered into my ear. Goose bumps covered my skin. I smiled and opened my eyes. Samuel's face was only a few inches above mine. I felt his warm breath. Boldly and with my heart pounding, I rose slightly to place a soft kiss on his cheek. He looked at me joyfully, grabbed my backpack, and reached out his hand. I didn't flinch as I took it.

I insisted on doing our laundry before checking in at the hotel. I didn't want the concierge to take care of it, because it would mean an extra expense. Samuel had talked me out of a hostel once again. He didn't have to try too hard this time.

"I didn't know I'd brought these sexy underpants." Samuel was unloading his washing machine, and I was busy emptying my own. When I finished, I turned around and saw him posing with my red lace panties held up against him. Oh my god! I wanted to disappear from the face of the earth.

"Seems like these belong to you," he laughed. I blushed. My face was as red as the panties that Samuel now twirled above his head. I began to sweat. The other people in the Laundromat looked over at us.

"Give them to me," I hissed, only half amused. He grinned. Desperately, I tried to grab the hand that held the bits of lace. I leaned against his chest and felt every muscle contract under my touch. Samuel's heart beat faster and so did mine. I stood on tiptoe, but he was simply too tall for me to grab my underwear. He raised his arm higher, and his laughter grew.

"Samuel, please," I implored. I was thankful the other people had become preoccupied with their own business again. I begged him again, then gave up. I lowered myself to my heels, crossed my arms over my chest, and just stared from under lowered brows at him. He looked so ridiculous that when he burst into song, I couldn't help but laugh at his pathetic performance. Tears of amusement rolled down my cheeks.

My cell phone interrupted our fun. I took it out of my skirt pocket, looked at the display, and declined the call. Seconds later, it sounded again, and again, I declined. When it went off a third time, I switched the setting to vibrate and shoved the phone back in my pocket.

"You sure you don't want to answer that?" Samuel asked.

I bit my lip. "I'd prefer not to."

Chapter 38
Samuel—Don't Switch Off

Marseille, July 2012

Mia's demeanor changed instantly. Her happy laughter disappeared as soon as she looked at her phone.

"It must be important. They've tried three times. And now it's ringing again."

She shook her head. But despite the running washers and dryers, I could clearly hear the vibrating sound. I cocked my head and looked at her.

"OK, you're right. It's ringing," she admitted. "But I'm not answering." She sounded stubborn. Testy.

I was sure the call was important. Why else would whoever it was be so insistent? Mia sat down on a folding chair and looked up at me. She seemed lost.

"It's just my mom," she said quietly.

"She knows you're traveling by train, right?" I inquired carefully.

"Both my parents do. But I want to be left alone."

There was more to it. Mia wasn't a good liar. Chewing her lip always gave her away.

"You should talk to them. Don't miss the opportunity. Things can change without warning."

"OK," she whispered.

After that, we drove to the hotel. I was shocked when Mia was the one to suggest sharing a room. "Are you serious?"

With her sweetest smile she answered, "Absolutely. I really don't want you to pay for two."

But her smile told me her decision wasn't about the money. Even if she made me sleep at the other end of the bed, she wanted me near her. And I wanted that, too. I wanted to spend as much time as possible with Mia. She distracted me from thinking too much about my own issues.

We spent the days in Marseille walking. A lot. Mia dragged me from one narrow alley to the next. She didn't seem to have a particular destination in mind, just a desire to find unusual places, off the beaten path. I'd never seen her smile so much. And she held my hand—often—squeezing it when she wanted to point out something. Her eyes sparkled. Her grin made my heart race. When we'd first met, I would have never imagined she could make me feel so happy. Gradually, her wall of self-protection was crumbling. She allowed more and more physical contact. I craved that contact. I had only to feel her fingers caress my skin, and arousal would grip my body. My muscles contracted. But I had to control myself. I knew she needed more time.

On the train to Toulouse, Mia sketched incessantly, a little frown appearing on her forehead as she concentrated. She drew, erased, grabbed her pencil again, drew again. Whenever I tried to catch a glimpse of her work in progress, she pressed the sketchbook tightly to her chest.

"Not even one little peek?"

"Not yet," she said.

I gave up and returned to plucking on my guitar. Her cell phone rang, interrupting us both.

"Damn it," Mia muttered and switched her phone to silent mode.

"Your mother?" I asked.

"Yes." The calls made her distressed and irritated. With one hand, she massaged her temple. The phone had been ringing every few hours, and she never answered. It was always someone from her family.

"Why don't you ever answer?" I couldn't understand. She'd told me how important her family was to her.

She sighed quietly. "You know, I was very attached to my parents and am very grateful for their support. But I need to put some distance between us." She sighed again. "They need to detach themselves from me even more."

When her cell sounded again, with a mix of desperation and something I couldn't quite put my finger on, she studied the screen. She leaned her head back. Closed her eyes. And answered.

"Christoph?" she said.

The conversation seemed very one-sided; Mia didn't say much.

"Yes, I'm doing fine. Really fine." She looked at me and blushed. "Extremely fine," she repeated in a softer voice. Her eyes were sparkling.

"No, Christoph, I don't want to. I should have known they're in touch with you. What did they want?" She clenched her hand into a fist around the phone.

"No, Chris, please . . . No. There is nothing to talk about." She sighed. "Very sure." Then she hung up. She propped her head in her hands, her elbows on her knees. I carefully touched her shoulder. She flinched, but after she tilted her head to look into my eyes, she finally relaxed and leaned against me. I didn't know who Christoph was or what he wanted—Mia had never mentioned him. But since talking to him, she seemed to have reverted to the Mia I'd met on the train to Budapest. Scared and upset.

She remained silent for the rest of the trip, plugged in her earbuds, and sank deep into her seat. After that moment of leaning against me, she'd moved away, and there was no more physical contact between us. She didn't speak. She didn't even look at me. She bit her fingernails and picked her cuticle. I wanted to stop her by reaching out my hand, but she flinched away. Her barriers were back up.

Later, in our hotel room, she tossed her backpack in the corner, then huddled on the bed. Every time I tried to talk to her, she cut me off. Every time I tried to touch her, she winced away and shot me an angry look. There had to be a way through to her! I had found it once. If I only knew what was going on. One short phone conversation had thrown her back into her old patterns. The same patterns she'd told me she wanted to change.

Wanting to stroke her hair, I squatted beside the bed instead, but when Mia didn't even react to my presence, I gave up.

I sighed. "I'm going out to walk around the block for a bit."

She didn't even look over at me. She just nodded, her head buried in the pillows.

Chapter 39
Mia—Selfish

Toulouse, July 2012

I should have known better than to answer the phone. I was such an idiot. But it was a matter of habit. Christoph's name appeared in the display; I hit the green button. How stupid. I should have guessed he was in cahoots with my parents, even though they weren't on speaking terms with each other after he dumped me. But desperate times called for desperate measures. And I certainly did not want to speak to my mother, father, or sister. This was my life. They didn't get to intrude. I'd hoped I could convince Christoph I was doing fine. Until a few hours ago, I'd thought I could put the past behind me and enjoy what remained for me.

Now I wasn't sure anymore that going forward with Samuel was the right thing to do. Maybe I should go home so I wouldn't end up hurting him more. But he made me feel so alive. I didn't want to let that sensation go. With each touch, he lit a fire in me that was growing stronger every day. I didn't want the flames to die. Maybe it was time to be selfish, for once. No matter what happened. What counted was I could feel alive again, if only for a short time.

It was difficult to treat my family this way. But it seemed like the best solution. I knew they would forgive me someday . . .

My headache returned, reminding me I was not healthy at all. I felt especially bad that day. I rolled over onto my back and stared at the ceiling, massaging my temples with my fingers. It didn't help the pain much, but it eased the worst of it.

A loud squeak sounded, and I bolted upright. I must have fallen asleep.

"I'm sorry, I didn't mean to wake you. But this damned door—" Samuel motioned to the bathroom behind him. Half-awake now, I rubbed my eyes. Samuel was wearing only his boxers. Water dripped from his hair. I couldn't stop looking at his incredibly toned abs and the line of dark hair harrowing down below his belly button. His shorts hung low on his hips. I swallowed hard and pulled my gaze away.

"I'll grab a sheet and sleep on the couch," he said.

"No," I protested. "Please, come here." He didn't move. "Please." I hoped my eyes implored him.

"OK. . ." Sounding uncertain, Samuel tossed the towel into the bathroom and slowly approached the bed. Reaching it, he hesitated.

"You can sit down." He sat as close as possible to the edge. I reached out my hand and waited for Samuel to take it. He seemed unsure whether he should touch me or not. No wonder, after I had pushed him away earlier. But I'd had to sort out my thoughts. I still wasn't certain I'd made the right decision.

I smiled, hoping to convince him everything was fine between us. Cautiously, he put his hand in mine. As soon as he touched me, warmth filled my body. I intertwined our fingers and leaned in closer. His eyes scanned my face, from my hair to my lips, then they roamed over my breasts, down to my belly and then my legs. I could see a faint smile. My heart beat a tattoo against my rib cage. For the first time, I enjoyed the heat in his gaze. The intimacy. This moment belonged to us. Our gazes locked. I inhaled deeply. "I needed time to think."

"Because of that call?" For the first time since we met, he sounded tentative. He always seemed so strong. At peace with himself. Cheerful.

"The call . . . It was Christoph." I played with Samuel's fingers. "He's the ex I told you about."

"You still answer that guy's calls?"

"Old habit," I said. "I know. It was stupid. Who would do that, right?"

We were sitting, facing each other. Samuel took my other hand.

I continued, "He reminded me of something I don't want to ever think about again. I want to forget. Not waste a single thought."

"What do you want to forget?"

I didn't want to tell him.

"Does it have anything to do with your mother's call?" He worded his question very carefully. After my behavior that afternoon, he was on guard. He'd managed to climb over the barricade I'd erected and find a place in my heart, and then, after one call, I'd pushed him away again. Maybe it was finally registering on him that I was crazy, after all.

He sighed. "Sweetie, you can tell me. I want you to be better. Do you really think burying how you're feeling will help?"

"Yes," I answered quietly. "Please don't ask me again."

"All right." He flashed me his sweetest smile. "Come closer."

My heart was still careening around in my chest. I let go of his hands and wrapped my arms around his neck. He whispered in my ear, "I want to be here for you. Even if I haven't known you for a long time. I want you to be happy. I want you to live."

This made me swallow hard. I looked into his eyes and saw pain and despair in them. "I want you to live," he repeated. His warm breath brushed my lips. I moistened them with the tip of my tongue. His hands, which until now had rested on my hips, moved slowly and gently up my sides. My breath caught and I squeezed my eyes shut.

He pulled back from the caress. "Too much?"

"No," I assured him. He cupped my face and leaned his forehead against mine. "Samuel," I whispered. Our lips touched briefly.

"Mia . . ."

I reached out and pulled him closer. With one hand tucked between us, I caressed his bare chest and felt the rapid beat of his heart. His lips covered mine, then his tongue slipped along my lower lip, and I let my mouth open. I could taste the peppermint flavor of his toothpaste as our tongues danced together. Samuel's hands caressed my back, and then they slipped under my T-shirt. Where they paused, waiting. Goose bumps broke out all over my flesh, and then there was fire. Only fire. Ignited by his touch. I shivered. The emotions raging inside me were new, strange. I wanted more. With a longing that grew so strong I couldn't hold back anymore. I quit resisting and let it take over.

Our kiss grew ravenous. He pulled me onto his lap. My trembling arms fell around his neck, and my fingers sank deep into his dark, wavy hair. Tenderly, he stroked my naked thighs. My lusty moans must have heightened Sam's arousal even more, as I felt his erection grow, press against me. His grip now strong, tight, he pulled me back with him until we were fully lying on the bed. My heart drummed in my ears.

Breathless, I interrupted the kiss. In one swift motion, I rolled off him, swung my legs out, and sat up on the edge of the bed. Although he'd been as careful as he could, the sensations were too much all at once. Too fast. I gasped for air.

Gently, Samuel wrapped his arms around my waist. "Breathe."

I inhaled, then twisted to look at him. His expression changed from worried to relieved, and he moved around to sit beside me. I took his hand and kissed his fingers.

"We just need to take it slower, easier," I whispered.

"No problem." He pulled me close to his side. I leaned my head against his shoulder, and we slowly settled back onto the mattress. I nuzzled into his chest. He brushed his lips across my forehead, and I closed my eyes, my pulse returning to normal. Soon I heard only Sam's steady heartbeat. "Really, it's not a problem at all, sweetie," he whispered again. "Sleep tight."

Chapter 40
Mia—Morale Booster

Toulouse, July 2012

I woke up next to Samuel. His arm was still wrapped around me as it'd been when I'd fallen asleep. I watched him slumber. He looked content. At peace. I hoped I was doing the right thing; it all felt so perfect. But I didn't want to hurt him.

I ran my fingertips across his naked chest, which rose and fell gently. I never would have imagined this could feel so good. Slowly, I caressed his throat and ran fingers through his beard, which tickled me when we kissed, then across his mouth. Sam opened his lips and drew in my finger. Oh wow . . . That stirred up things down below. My skin prickled as arousal overtook me.

Sam opened his eyes and grinned at me. As my hand fell, he captured it with his and kissed my fingertips.

"Good morning," he said in a sleepy voice. He yawned and rubbed his eyes. "What time is it?"

"Far too early. The sun is just about to rise," I whispered. "I didn't want to wake you."

"No worries. Did you have bad dreams?"

I shook my head.

Still he eyed me. "Is everything OK?"

I smiled. "Absolutely." I propped up on my elbows to better look at him. "Actually, I was having *sweet* dreams. Maybe that's why I woke up." I rarely remembered my dreams, though I knew when I'd had nightmares, because I woke up startled or worse, my heart racing.

"Sweet dreams, eh?"

I nodded and kissed his shoulder.

"What about?" His warm breath against my ear made my flesh tingle. Instead of an answer, I lowered my head and kissed, then suckled the skin of his throat. Softly, he gripped my waist to pull me closer. I kissed my way up to his lips. With an intensity equal to the degree of hatred I'd once felt for him for being a Winter, I wanted to make love with him now. I could no longer resist the chemistry between us and silenced my conscience, which protested I'd only hurt Samuel if I let this go further. I didn't want to listen. I wanted only to revel in him.

Carefully, he answered my kiss. His hands wandered up my bared back until they slipped into the hair on my nape. Our kiss deepened. I stroked his arms, his shoulders. Heat built inside me, and the fluttering was back in my stomach. My heart was pounding.

I felt Samuel smile against my lips. Dreamily, I pulled away to look up at him, biting my lower lip. He bent his head and placed a tender kiss there, forcing me to stop.

"I've wanted to do this since the day I first saw you torture this perfect lip." His smile grew broader, and his gray eyes shone. "Do you have any idea how hot it makes me when you do that?"

"No," I whispered and bit my lip again.

Samuel ran his tongue over his lips, then devoured my mouth. I wanted more. I positioned myself on top of him. His breath caught, and he looked into my eyes, silently asking whether I was truly ready. His hands fell to my legs, and he caressed the soft flesh of my inner thighs with his thumbs as they slowly moved up to my hips. Head back, I was breathing heavily now. Then his touch moved to my belly. Hastily, I grabbed his wrists.

"Stop," I gasped. "Please don't go further there." His hands dropped to lay loose on my legs. With my eyes on his, I drew his gaze to the scar on my arm and finally to my belly.

"May I see what you're hiding?" he asked carefully. "I'll keep my hands where they are now. Don't worry. I won't touch you where you don't want to be touched. Just let me know."

"Thank you," I whispered.

I kept my eyes on his while I lifted my shirt. The scar was long and had healed poorly. The marks from the surgical staples were visible. How I hated this scar. It reminded me every day that nothing was OK.

"Thank you," Samuel said quietly. Quickly, I covered my belly again with my shirt. Samuel sat up, with me still on top of him, and folded his arms around me. "Thank you," he said again and kissed my forehead. I leaned my brow against his.

Just then, my phone rang. With a few smooth movements, I grabbed it from the bedside table and declined the call.

Samuel stroked my hair. "Maybe it's something important."

I shook my head. "I know it's not."

He snorted. "It's your business. All I'm saying is it's really important to stay in touch with people you love, especially your parents." He looked at me with sad eyes. I thought I saw a glimmer of tears, but he quickly turned his head. "Talk with them before it's too late."

I wasn't sure I understood what he meant.

Chapter 41
Samuel—I Want More

En route to Biarritz, July 2012

"Biarritz?" she'd asked.

"Yes, Biarritz," I said and stroked my thumb over her hand. We were sitting on the train.

"Never heard of it," she replied. "We're still in France, though, right?"

I laughed. "Yes, still in France. You wanted to travel. Let me be your guide."

Mia leaned against my shoulder. "Well, well, Mr. Tour Guide. What will we be doing in Biarritz?" She kissed my cheek. Those soft lips on my skin always made my heart beat faster.

"It's pronounced *bee-yah-rits*," I corrected.

"See? I can't even say it right."

I chuckled.

Playfully, she tapped my upper arm. "And now you're laughing at me." She had to suppress her own grin.

"I would never dare do that," I whispered against her lips and gave her a kiss. She leaned back and yawned. "Am I so boring?" I asked.

Mia covered her mouth with one hand and yawned again. "You know you're not. But I'm exhausted."

"You have enough time to take a nap."

"And that I will do. But first, you go sit over there." She pointed at the seats across from ours.

I raised my eyebrows. "You've already had enough of me?"

"Never, Samuel Winter. But I need you to serenade me." She couldn't hide a smile.

I answered her smile, kissed the tip of her nose, then her forehead. "With pleasure."

It took only one song for Mia to drop off. When she slept, she looked at peace, her face free of worry lines. She looked younger. Free. Even I felt calmer as I watched her.

I definitely worried about her, though. Although she seemed happy most of the time now, she wasn't—not really. I could tell something weighed on her. Something she wouldn't reveal. I suspected whatever it was had to do with her parents. They were still trying to reach her.

I didn't know her well enough to question her decisions. This one made me wonder, though. From my own experience, I knew Mia would regret if something happened to one of them, and she'd continued to refuse their calls. I could only hope she knew what she was doing. I was still beating myself up for not picking up the phone that day in my own past when I should have.

Shortly before we arrived in Biarritz, I woke up Mia by whispering her name in her ear. It had become our ritual. I loved watching a smile play on her lips before she opened her eyes. She reached out an arm so I could help her to her feet.

"Thank you," she murmured.

At the station, we hailed a cab and drove to the hotel I'd reserved while we were still in Toulouse. Mia didn't complain anymore. Youth hostels were no longer mentioned, now that she'd spent a few nights in comfortable beds. She didn't need to worry about the money; the room rate was no different if I paid for one person or two. But she insisted she'd pay back every cent of her share.

As soon as we were in our room, she fell onto the mattress, still wearing her backpack. "Can we stay in?" she said through a yawn. "I'd rather relax. I can't even keep my eyes open." She snuggled into the pillows.

"Sure. Wouldn't it be more comfortable, though, if you take that thing off? And maybe some clothes?"

Mia sat up. "Take off some clothes? That's what's on your mind?"

Oh damn . . .

"Um, uh, no. No, that's not what I meant," I stammered. Of course I wanted to . . . When she touched me with her fingertips, my whole body tingled. But of course I'd only make love to her if she wanted to, too. "I mean . . . Oh, forget it." I hit my forehead with my palm. I didn't want her to think I was after only sex.

Suddenly, she was standing in front of me, tenderly holding my wrists.

"I know what you meant. Don't sweat it." She kissed both my palms. Then she stood on tiptoe, kissed the end of my nose, and whispered in my ear, "You'll know when I'm ready."

She grimaced when she shifted her weight back onto her heels, even swayed a bit.

I grasped her arm. "Are you OK?"

"Oh yes." She smiled at me guardedly as she moved to the bed. "I just want to relax, that's all. After spending an entire year at home, I'm just not used to traveling this much. I'll be in good shape tomorrow, and you can show me Biarritz."

"All right." I gave her a kiss. "You're already pronouncing Biarritz much better," I teased.

Without further conversation, she huddled under the sheets and was quickly asleep.

I was agitated, restless. For hours, I lay awake next to her, trying to decide how far I should travel with her. There was something I had to take care of. Something I needed to do alone.

Chapter 42
Mia—Life Is Beautiful

Biarritz, July 2012

Unfortunately, my headache wasn't entirely gone the next morning. I could still feel a dull throbbing. Hardly surprising, what with the hot temperatures where we were.

Over breakfast, I asked Samuel, "So what does my tour guide have in store for us today? What do people do here?"

"Surfing." He smiled.

"S-surfing?" I stammered. "I've never done that. And I don't really like to show a lot of skin in public." I grew tense. No, going to the beach was clearly not a good idea. I began folding and unfolding my napkin.

Sam covered my hand with his and stroked the back with his thumb. "Hey, we won't actually go surfing, sweetie. I don't know how, myself. We'll just watch, if you like. I think a day at the beach would do us good, don't you?"

We'd walked on the beaches in Nice, so OK, I could probably survive a full day at one, too. As long as I didn't go into the water. I wouldn't look too ridiculous sitting on the beach in a light tunic shirt. I nodded reluctantly. Samuel flashed a reassuring smile.

The beach was crowded. Overcrowded. I turned to Samuel. "Quiet day at the beach, eh?"

He scratched his head. "Um . . . well. I didn't expect this place to be so packed. We'll find a spot, though."

"No worries. I'll be fine," I said, not knowing whether I said the words to convince myself that the flocks of people didn't matter to me or to show Samuel I wasn't mad at him. Eventually, we found a spot big enough for our towel at the farthest end of the beach.

While I wasn't going to take off my shirt, I still asked Samuel to put cream on my back. His grin told me everything. He was craving an excuse to touch me, and the same was true for me. The faintest caress from him threw my body into turmoil.

He rolled up my white tunic very gently. "Hold it here so it doesn't fall down."

Very tenderly, he applied sunscreen on my back while placing soft kisses on my shoulders and neck. I had to squeeze my eyes shut to restrain myself from visibly reacting. Eventually, Samuel rolled down the shirt, moved closer, and pulled me to a seat between his stretched-out legs so I could lie back against him, and then rested his forearms on my naked thighs. He didn't stop kissing my neck.

"What's this perfume that smells like vanilla?" he murmured.

"I don't use perfume."

"A shower gel?"

"Why all these questions?" I twisted around to look into his eyes.

"You're not aware that you're emanating this incredibly enchanting vanilla aroma?"

A timid smile curled my lips, and I nuzzled closer into his embrace.

The afternoon flew by, although we didn't do much. We just sat and watched the sunbathers and surfers. Watched each other. We talked and then fell silent. We laughed and kissed. Everything seemed normal, routine. Like a perfect everyday routine

I liked that.

It was getting dark when Samuel took off his T-shirt. By then, we were lying on the beach, facing each other. I let my index finger trail down his chest to his belly button. I had totally fallen for those abs. Every night, I enjoyed feeling his muscles under my hand as I fell asleep with my head on his shoulder.

I heard Samuel catch his breath. His lowered eyes followed my movements.

"So, now you're showing me this?" I indicated his sculpted chest. "Now, when I can hardly see anything?"

"Who wants to see, when you can feel?" His voice was rough with desire. I snuggled closer, but he moved away. I looked at him, surprised. I made a second attempt, and he scooted back again. Then I saw his mischievous smile. He jumped to his feet and crossed his arms over his chest. Slowly, I rose, too, then took a step toward him. He took an equal step back.

"I guess you'll have to catch me," he joked, before turning and running off.

"Hey! That's not fair!" I yelled and ran after him as fast as I could, but, oh man, he was quite a sprinter. I would never catch up with him and was already out of breath. Pressing my palms against my thighs I let my head hang down, hoping it would be easier to breathe in this position. When I looked up, I didn't see Samuel anywhere.

"Samuel?" I called. Nothing. "Samuel, where are you?" Still no answer. Then suddenly two strong arms grabbed me from behind. I screamed. Samuel laughed in my ear.

"Don't scare me like that!" I slapped his arm, but he only laughed louder and ran off again. This time I was on his heels. I caught up with him and jumped on his back.

"This isn't the plan! But—" Samuel didn't put me down. Instead, he grabbed my knees and ran even faster. When I realized what he was up to, anxiety filled me.

"Samuel, no! No, don't do this!" I flailed and kicked, hoping he'd stop.

"You bet I'll do this!" We were nearing the water.

"No, no, no!" I shouted. I had a stranglehold on his neck and my legs gripped his waist. He raced straight into the surf, continuing until the waves washed over us.

Gasping for air, I surfaced. "Shit, it's freezing!" I said.

"Oh, come on. It's not that cold." Samuel was still grinning from ear to ear.

"I usually don't go into water where the temperature can't be adjusted. Look . . ." I stretched out my arm. "Goose bumps everywhere."

Water dripped from his hair, and he wiped his face. "Let me see." He took my hand and slowly kissed his way up my arm. When he reached my neck, he paused and tickled my ear with the tip of his tongue. It felt so wonderful I started to shiver. He nibbled on my lobe. I flung my arms around his neck so that I could pull him closer. "It's too dark to see goose bumps, so maybe I should try to feel them?" he whispered.

His tender kisses wandered across my cheek to my mouth. My blood raced. I put my hand over his heart and felt its steady rhythm. He leaned his forehead against mine. His right hand wrapped around my neck, and his thumb stroked my cheek.

"You are so amazingly beautiful, Mia," he whispered and looked deep into my eyes. His shone with excitement.

In my lowest voice, I murmured, "I wish I had met you sooner."

Chapter 43
Samuel—You Are Magnificent

Biarritz, July 2012

I wasn't sure I'd heard Mia correctly. Yet I didn't ask her to repeat her words, because I didn't want to ruin this amazing moment.

I bowed my head. She smiled, emanating a wonderful warmth even in the chill of the surf. She'd lowered her wall. For good, I hoped. I liked this version of Mia. She was a little shy but natural. Without her barriers, I could see how she really was—intelligent and stunning. She took my breath away.

"I'm going to kiss you now, Mia," I whispered.

She nodded, still smiling. I took her lips with mine and tasted the salt water from the ocean and the sweetness of her mouth. Her tongue slid out and circled my lower lip. I held her closer.

Our tongues danced. Every cell in my body went on high alert. Mia sighed and grabbed my hair, pulling me even closer. My erection pressed against her stomach. Again, she sighed. This was almost too hot.

I let my hands cradle her butt and lifted her up. She wrapped her legs around me. Our kiss deepened. Dizzy with wanting her, I paused. Mia touched her forehead to mine. She was breathing as heavily as I was.

"Let's go back to the hotel," I whispered. She nodded.

The hotel was only a short walk from the beach, and we ran all the way, laughing and holding hands. Mia had the towel wrapped around her, and I wore my now-soaked shirt. I held her fingers tight. A small puddle formed around our feet while we waited for the elevator in the lobby. Her continuing laughter sent shivers down my spine.

"They'll be so pleased with us for this mess," I said in a low voice. Giggling, she hid her face against my chest.

The elevator moved slowly upward. Once inside, Mia had grown quiet. Biting her lip again, she gave me a timid glance. I stroked my thumb over her mouth. She looked up at me with sparkling eyes.

"You're driving me crazy," I whispered and kissed her softly. Instantly, she wrapped her arms around my neck and threaded her fingers in my hair.

When the elevator doors opened, Mia let go, then tugged me toward our room. I opened the door as fast as I could. Once inside, I closed it with a kick of my foot. Mia stood in front of me, the towel still wrapped around her body. Her chest was slowly rising and falling. We looked at each other. I drowned in her eyes. Then Mia let the towel glide down to the floor. Her white tunic shirt clung to her wet body; I could see her bra through the thin cloth—and all the contours of her body.

I pushed my wet hair back and finally came closer, putting both my hands on her hips. Mia leaned into my chest.

"You're trembling. Do you want to take a hot shower?"

She shook her head and took a few steps backward. Slowly, she lifted the hem of her blouse and pulled it over her head. My eyes wandered over her perfect body. I wanted more. I wanted it all. After she dropped the shirt on the floor, I took her hand and pulled her close again.

"You are magnificent." She blushed and ducked her head. I lifted her chin with my index finger. "Mia, really, you are so beautiful."

"Thank you," she whispered. Then she stood on tiptoe and gave me a kiss. I held her close. She deepened the kiss, and I pulled her tight against me. Her hands wandered across my back and stopped at the hem of my shirt. I felt her cold fingers slip underneath, to my naked skin, and my flesh prickled. She started to lift the shirt, and I could feel her trembling. Reaching behind me, I grasped her wrist.

"Mia, you don't need to do this," I said.

She whispered in my ear, "What if I want to?"

My breath caught. I didn't need to hear more. I helped her rid me of my shirt. With a fingertip, she traced an invisible line from my shoulder to my belly button.

I led her to the bed. Lowering herself onto her back, she edged up until her head reached the headboard. I settled myself beside her, then lavished her with kisses. On the tip of her nose. Her mouth. Up her neck. I let my tongue glide over the softest skin I had ever felt. Drift over her collarbone. I placed a kiss over her heart. Kissed a path down between her breasts.

She sighed softly, which aroused me even more. Her body arched under my touch. She gripped my hair. When my mouth neared the big scar on her right side, I paused and looked up at her. I wanted to ask how far she would allow me to go. Her eyes were squeezed tight, and she was frowning.

"I can stop, if you want me to," I said. She opened her eyes, and I could see the panic in their depths. "Breathe, Mia. I won't continue if you tell me to stop."

Mia took a deep breath. "No . . ." Her voice trembled. "I want to feel." I rose up to study her more closely. "Samuel, will you be careful?"

I nodded. "Of course. Always. Just tell me if it gets to be too much, OK?"

"OK."

Chapter 44
Mia—I Want To Feel Me

Biarritz, July 2012

I was afraid. It had been a long time since I'd been intimate with a man. My entire body trembled. I was so tense. My chest would have burst had my heart beat any faster. Everything was new, as if I were experiencing this for the first time in my life. Strange feelings rushed through me. Cold . . . warmth . . . desire . . . lust . . . craving . . .

The only thing I knew for sure was that I wanted more. To the same degree I was afraid of this situation, I longed for it, too. Samuel was only kissing me, but it meant so much more. I could feel it. My body felt it.

Samuel was gentle, and like he'd promised, didn't go near my scar.

His lips touched my skin for brief moments. He kissed me, then withdrew before finding a new and sensitive spot to place his mouth, which ignited my passion until my whole body quivered, fear and lust mingling.

Sam slid back up until he was nuzzling my neck.

I put my hands on his shoulders. "Samuel?" He raised his head. "I want to feel." His expression turned puzzled. "I want to feel your lips on my stomach." He sucked in a breath. I wanted his kisses and his fingers on the scar. "I want to feel," I whispered again.

He asked with his eyes if I meant it, and I nodded. Then I felt two of his fingers glide gently over my collarbone, then along the valley between my breasts. His touch made me shiver, and I gasped. His fingers were close now. I screwed my eyes shut.

"Don't forget to breathe, Mia," he said. I could still feel the warm line of the path he'd traced. He circled my belly button with one finger. Slid down my body to kiss there, as well.

"Open your eyes." I did. "Take my hand." I obeyed him again. "Guide me."

I held his wrist and moved our hands until they hovered over my abdomen. I guided him until his fingertips could just barely reach my skin. I felt his warmth. The softness of his flesh. I smiled. Samuel's eyes shone brightly. It was OK, because I was in control. I brushed his fingers along the scar. I could feel. I was allowed to feel. I was happy.

I was feeling...

"Stretch out your fingers." One of his hands now rested flat on my belly. I put mine on top.

"Thank you for trusting me," he whispered.

I tugged on him until he brought his face near mine. The chemistry between us was almost too much to endure. I felt a fire burning inside me. Samuel's eyes mirrored the same feeling. It was not only lust. We were attracted by *something else*. Something I couldn't quite grasp. Something I'd never experienced until this moment. I thought I had experienced *it* before. But I hadn't. This was the real thing.

Our lips found each other's. Samuel rolled onto his back and positioned me so I was sitting on top of him. His erection pressed against my entrance as I moved against his pelvis. My fingers ran down his chest to his still-sea-damp shorts. My thumbs reached the waistband at the same time he opened my bikini top. He pushed the straps over my shoulders and discarded the scrap of cloth. Raising his head he pulled my torso toward him until, hungrily, he could lick circles around my nipples. I shuddered. The heat inside me burned brighter. Sam flicked his tongue, alternating nipples and, finally, drew one in to suckle. I was no longer in control of my body. My back arched. I moaned.

"Oh, Mia, you taste so goddamn wonderful. I want more," he said. Softly he pushed me back, then drew himself up on his knees to kiss his way down my belly until he reached my shorts. He opened the placket. My heart beat faster. He undid the zipper and tugged down the pants until I could kick them aside, then let his fingers trace along the waistband of my bikini panties. I tingled—everywhere. Samuel ran his mouth along my inner thighs. Then slowly, gradually, he pulled down my panties.

"Mia . . ." he said in a muffled voice. His warm breath tickled my skin.

"Take off your clothes," I moaned.

In short order, he stood naked beside the bed. I admired him. His broad shoulders, his hard chest. His toned abs.

Very carefully, he lowered himself until he'd covered my body with his. I took his face between my hands and pulled him to me. I needed to feel his soft lips on mine.

A rough sigh escaped from deep in his chest. He shifted. Tenderly, he ran a hand up my leg, making me shiver anew. His fingertips came closer and closer to my entrance. My heart beat fast, loud in my ears. The heat built inside me. *Move up higher . . .*

He paused, then thrust two fingers into my warmth. My body was ready for him. I was nearly whimpering with desire.

"Oh wow . . ." he rasped out. His thumb circled my clitoris.

"Sam," I whispered. "I want to feel you."

He withdrew his skillful fingers, spread my legs, and penetrated me, gently, carefully. The sensation was overwhelming. We moved in rhythm with each other. I wrapped my legs tight around his hips so that he could thrust deeper inside me. Making soft guttural sounds in my ear, he kissed my neck. I scratched my nails over his back, and when the heat surged, I dug them into his skin.

Then I let go.

We climaxed at almost the same time. And when we were done, we looked at each other, out of breath and with hearts still pounding. I lost myself in the gray depths of his eyes.

"I've never felt like this before," I whispered. "Alive. Happy." I softly kissed his mouth.

Samuel stroked my hair. "I've never been allowed to feel like this."

He rolled onto his side and drew me against him. Then he pulled up the sheets and held me tight in his arms.

Chapter 45

Mia—I Feel Incredible

Bordeaux, July 2012

I never wanted to leave Biarritz. It was so wonderful here. Even though the crowds had frightened me on the first day at the beach, I now wanted to return. Samuel had made me feel confident enough to expose my body. The longer I was with him, the more comfortable I felt with myself and my appearance. In fact, I felt incredible. Samuel had rekindled that long-lost aspect of my personality and ignited so much more. I couldn't believe it. I actually felt good. I could look in the mirror. Really look at myself. I touched my hair. It was short, but with Kriszta's cut I actually looked . . . pretty. I didn't need a hat anymore.

"What are you doing?" Samuel's voice startled me. I had been so lost in my thoughts that I hadn't even noticed he'd entered the bathroom. I turned from the mirror.

"Feeling good," I said and put my arms around his waist.

He tilted his head and gave me a puzzled look. "You were just looking at yourself in the mirror, and your answer is *feeling good*?"

"I could look at myself and actually think I look fine. I owe that to you." I kissed his cheek.

He smiled. "I don't know what I did, but I like that you've been beaming all day." He nuzzled my forehead with his lips.

"It's all because you're here with me," I replied. "I would have never gone to that beach alone. But you give me strength and make me feel special." *If only for a short time*, I thought.

"That's what you are, Mia. Special. I knew it from the moment I saw you."

I leaned against him and let him hold me for a long time.

Samuel played his guitar for me every night. I loved listening to him, and I couldn't resist singing along—timid and with a low voice at first, but then he encouraged me to really get into it. So I did. He was the only one who would hear me, anyway. Every time I chimed in, he flashed me the sweetest smile, and I'd feel a burst of joy. It was impossible to say where I would be now had I not met Samuel. Or what would have happened had I ignored him. I was glad I hadn't been able to. He was irresistible, and we were intensely attracted to each other. We belonged together.

I couldn't imagine life without him. One thing concerned me, though. What would happen to him when I left? Inevitably, I would one day be gone. Reality was gradually catching up with me. My parents. My sister. Christoph. Even Julia regularly called me.

I should have just switched off the phone entirely. I don't know why I didn't. Maybe I wanted to see that everyone at home loved me that much. Maybe I needed proof they were still thinking of me. Maybe I would have eventually been able to answer.

Maybe . . .

Samuel tried to persuade me to let them know I was OK, even if only in a text.

"Mia," he sighed over lunch in Bordeaux. "Please don't be so stubborn. I'm sure they need to speak with you. No matter what happened between you, put it aside and talk to them."

The big lump in my throat was back. I couldn't swallow another bite. I put down my utensils, rubbed my face, and ran my fingers through my hair. "I can't, Samuel. Believe me. It . . ." I swallowed hard. "It would . . . I don't know. It would hurt them. Or they would freak out."

Samuel put his hand on mine. "What is it you can't tell them?"

"They probably found out that I don't plan to go back. I—I just don't want to return, that's all. I need to find a new place."

Samuel squeezed my hand and gave me an encouraging look. He seemed to understand what I was talking about. After all, he, too, had left his home to escape his daily life. I wasn't the only one looking for change.

"Even if you can't go back or don't want to go back . . . Talk to them."

Maybe. But I wasn't ready yet.

Our trip took us farther north. It seemed that with each mile we traveled, Samuel's mood grew more pensive.

"Is everything OK with you?" I asked while standing in front of the castle in Nantes.

He pulled me close and kissed my forehead. "Yep, all is well. I was only thinking about where we should go next, and when."

"We just got here. I'd like to stay at least a day. I mean, look at this." I pointed at the castle. "This must be even more fascinating for you than it is for me."

Samuel rested his hands on my waist. "Right now, there's only one thing I find fascinating. Or rather, one person." He lowered his head and kissed me passionately. I gripped his shoulders as my knees grew weak. With each kiss and each touch, I craved him even more.

I really liked this man. Maybe too much. That scared me, weighed on me. Then I remembered a conversation I'd had with Dr. Weiß.

Chapter 45 ½
Mia—Let Go

Graz, October 2011

"You need to let go," Dr. Weiß said. But I couldn't. Everything had to remain shut away. Otherwise I would break down. After the emotional turmoil in August, I had sworn nobody would ever get that close to me again. Never again . . .

Not my family, let alone a man. Yet everyone insisted on intruding on my world.

We only want to help you, Mia. Nobody could help me.

"Mia, you are allowed to cry. You are allowed to feel. Rage, anger, grief . . . Let it all out, otherwise it will eat you alive. There will be a day when you won't be able to keep your mask on anymore. It will start to slip."

"No, Dr. Weiß, it won't. And *nobody* will get behind it. That includes you," I snapped.

"Maybe I won't. I can't say. We hardly know each other yet. But let me tell you that there will come a time when it does, and you won't even notice it's happening."

"And then what?" I crossed my arms over my chest, not believing him.

"Why, you'll feel again," he said.

"I've had more than my share of feeling. I've felt things nobody wants to experience."

"How can I show you that everything you're going through is absolutely normal?" He said it quietly, but I heard him. "One day, it all will change. You can't prevent that. Don't even try. So be selfish and let your feelings run freely. It doesn't matter for how long . . . Just allow it to happen," he said.

I didn't want to listen to him. I didn't want to see him. I closed my eyes.

"You are crushing your emotions. Set them free. Then they won't crush you."

Chapter 46
Mia—Unspoken Feelings

Nantes, July 2012

I interrupted our kiss and grasped Samuel's shoulders. Air... I needed air. Those feelings must not crush me. My therapist had been right all along. I couldn't prevent this *something* I shared with Samuel from happening. It was too strong. My heart longed for him too much. My body longed for his touch too much. I couldn't do anything but let go and live it, although I knew there would be no happy ending for us.

I gasped for oxygen. I felt dizzy.

"Mia?" Samuel sounded worried.

"I—I—" I stammered and took another deep breath. "I just forgot to breathe. Everything's fine. You're just too overwhelming."

"How so?" Samuel pulled me closer.

I tried to smile and said, "So." I kissed his full lips.

Amidst all the tourists, Samuel lifted me up so abruptly that I shrieked. He spun us around, and I couldn't help but laugh. After a few turns he put me back on my feet.

"Please hold me," I said, laughing. "You definitely twirled me too much."

"You mean like this?"

I was back in his arms, and I buried my face against his chest. "Please, let me down. Everyone is staring at us," I said against his T-shirt.

"Oh, that's just your imagination. Even if they are, who cares? I'm enjoying the moment with you."

His whispered words sent a shiver down my spine. He lightly kissed the top of my head. I looked at him and laughed. He was right. It was nobody's business, so why care? I should enjoy the moment. Samuel and what we had was well worth a little embarrassment. He made me feel alive. Made me forget the past.

Sam lowered me to the ground but continued holding me and nibbled lightly on my shoulder. My body reacted instantly. "So, where were we?"

My hands wandered over his impressive chest up to his neck. "Let's go," I whispered.

"Your place or mine?" he asked jokingly.

I poked his upper arm. "As if I had a choice. You won't let me have my own room."

With a broad grin, he took my hand and dragged me along. At the hotel, he unlocked our door and walked in ahead of me. I leaned against the door frame and watched him.

"What's the matter?" he asked. "You're not coming in?"

When I still didn't move, he returned to me, took my hand, and led me inside.

"I would have been happy just standing there and watching you for the rest of the day," I said. Samuel kissed my forehead. "I can't get enough of you." I took his hand and placed it on my chest. "Here, feel." My heart was strong and steady when I looked into his eyes. "I can't remember when it last beat like that." Now that I was sharing my feelings, I wanted to let him know.

Samuel took my hand and put it on those pecs I loved so much. "Here, feel mine," he said quietly. "It's the same. This is all new to me, these unknown emotions . . . I like them." He paused. "I like *you*, Mia."

I raised my mouth to his. I was hungry for him. Together, we fell onto the bed. I appreciated how gentle Samuel was with me. Our lovemaking seemed to take place in slow-motion. After every button he opened, he gave me a kiss. I sat up, tugged his shirt, one the same gray as his eyes, over his head, and simply stared at him. He stared back, as intently as me, not saying a word. There was so much tension between us. So many unspoken feelings. His every touch made my skin tingle. Countless butterflies swarmed in my stomach. I was melting. I was forgetting.

Sam undressed me and grinned. "Ah, there are the red panties again. I've missed them. Couldn't find them in my bag."

"If you really want them so badly, why don't you come get them?" I teased.

"With pleasure," he mumbled and tongued my belly, making sure not to touch the scar. He pulled down the red lace.

"Have I mentioned before that you look magnificent?"

I felt heat rush to my cheeks and singe my entire body.

"The color in your face suits you," he whispered.

After he rose, I ran my hands down his chest to the button on his jeans. He helped me undress him.

"And have I mentioned I love seeing you like this?"

I put my arms on his shoulders and gently pushed him back onto the bed. I covered his chest with kisses as light as down and felt his body tense under my touch. Then he took command. He stroked me everywhere. Kissed me everywhere. He was demanding, yet gentle.

I straddled him, raising and lowering my pelvis to his. Samuel held my hips, controlling the pace of my movements. The friction of our naked bodies sent us soaring, and finally climax took us. Then we collapsed, breathing heavy, hearts racing, Samuel's pounding against my own. He was as fulfilled, spent, and overwhelmed as I was.

He rested his head against my shoulder as his hands caressed my back. I held him close. I never wanted to let him go.

"I live through you, Mia," I heard him say quietly.

Chapter 47
Mia—Just a Game

Paris, July 2012

I fell in love with Paris immediately. I'd always wanted to visit the city, and I'd now spent two days in its splendor with a man I really liked. A man who, after only a short time, had reached me like nobody had before. A man who had turned my life upside down. He was right when he'd said *I live through you.* I was living through him, as well.

There were so many things I wanted to experience in Paris. The Louvre and Mona Lisa—not as a postcard or online but right in front of me! Climbing the Eiffel Tower. Taking in the stunning view of the starlike pattern of streets radiating from the Arc de Triomphe, with the Eiffel Tower in the distance. The Pantheon! Seeing the sun rise over the Basilica of the Sacred Heart in Montmartre. I wanted to stroll from one cafe to the next every evening, with Samuel by my side.

Unfortunately, this plan was too far-reaching. Or rather, my time was too short.

One evening, I dressed in the prettiest clothes I had in my backpack.

"Wow, sweetie, you look amazing." Samuel leaned against the bathroom door while I tried to do something different with my hair. I still wasn't used to having it this short.

"Leave it as it is," he said. "It's perfect. Trust me."

I sighed and turned. He looked amazing in his gray T-shirt, with a dark blue vest, perfectly fitting jeans, and brown leather shoes. I hadn't seen him wearing this particular outfit.

I hugged him. "Likewise. You look dressed up for a change. No faded shirts and hoodies."

Samuel wrapped his arms around me. "Well, well, so you don't like my shirts and my hoodies? Why do you always borrow them then?"

"Because they smell like you," I whispered against his lips and kissed him. His response was intense and heated.

But I slipped out of his embrace. "If we continue like this, we'll never make it to that nice cafe we saw." I gave a mournful sigh and walked out of his reach.

Smiling, Sam leaned against the door frame and watched me put on my ballerina flats.

"Ready when you are."

He took my hand and, shortly, we were stepping out onto the street.

The night had grown cool, and I snuggled against Samuel while we wandered through the streets along the river. The lights twinkled on the Seine. I had always known I would love it here; it was like being in a fairy tale. When rain began to fall, Samuel pulled me closer and sheltered me in his strong arms.

"Let's hurry, or we'll get wet."

Suddenly, my cell phone vibrated in my bag. He could feel it, too, because we were pressed so close together. When I didn't reach for it, he stopped.

"Come on, Mia. Are you going to answer this call, or what?" My family didn't call as often anymore, but they hadn't stopped altogether.

Tilting my head up toward Samuel, I pleaded with my eyes to let the subject drop once and for all. I would explain everything when I was ready.

"Mia," he sighed. "They obviously need to tell you something, and ignoring them isn't going to make them stop." He shook his head. I didn't understand why my lack of responsiveness bothered him so much. Why did he act as if it was his business, anyway?

His gaze was cutting right through me. I had to look away before he swayed me like he had before. If he couldn't, I wouldn't be standing here now, with him in Paris. If he hadn't convinced me otherwise, I would have never thought I'd have anything in common with a guy like Samuel Winter. A guy I would have never imagined would even want to find himself on a trip with me.

He sighed again. "Look at me."

I swallowed hard. No, I didn't want to. Too much could change. My heart began to race.

"Please, Mia." Samuel seemed sad. Depressed, even. I bit my lip and finally raised my eyes again. "Mia, I need to go to London." I looked at him, dumbfounded. That was not what I had expected to hear.

"Um, OK." The rain was falling harder now. Our plan had been to continue from here to Amsterdam, but if he wanted, I'd go to London instead. Being with him was all that mattered.

"I . . . I need to visit someone in London, in Fulham," he stammered. His fingers nervously toyed with mine. Strands of wet hair clung to his forehead, and he impatiently pushed them back.

"Oh." I retreated from his embrace. I should have known. "Who is she?" I said in an ice-cold voice.

Frowning, he stepped closer, but I kept out of his reach.

"What makes you think there's a *she*?"

I shook my head. "Sam, I'm not stupid. The farther north we've gotten, the more nervous you've become. You're stammering for a reason." I turned, wanting only to walk away. I shook with anger. My clothes, my pretty clothes, were soaked and clung to my body, and I was about to break down in tears. I wanted out of here. Out of here and out of this dress and into a warm shower. I should have known better, I should have known this was all just a game for him. But no. I *had* to follow my feelings. My heartbeat became a roar in my ears; I couldn't hear anything else. The headache descended with a vicious bang.

"Mia," he sighed. "It's not what you think it is."

I froze when I heard those words. *It's not what you think it is.* That same sentence had ended something good. Or rather, something I had assumed was good. Those words had destroyed what little had been left of my desire to live. I wouldn't go there again. Samuel was just a flirt, I repeated. If he could play games, so could I. I was not going to suffer like I had before.

I inhaled deeply and pushed the emotions aside. "No worries."

"Sweetie—"

"Don't call me *sweetie*." I gathered all the courage I had. "Really, Samuel, it's no big deal. I'll come with you if you want."

"OK," he said quietly.

"Let's go back. I'm freezing."

Chapter 48
Samuel—I Have to Let Her Go

Paris, July 2012

Mia wouldn't listen. She was acting completely stubborn, not like the brave and free-spirited woman I'd learned to care so much about, a Mia without barricades. I didn't want the situation to escalate and so damage her newfound courage. I needed to clear my head first before I dealt with it.

On our way back, she didn't say a word. Her arms remained crossed defensively over her chest as she marched to the hotel. Her body shook, I assumed with anger and not just cold. I wanted to put my arm around her, but she'd have none of it and pushed me away.

It was still pouring. We were completely drenched by the time we arrived back at our room.

"Let me help you."

"I can take off my dress myself, Sam."

I flinched when I heard her call me Sam. On the way to Budapest, I had introduced myself by my nickname but had later asked her to call me Samuel. I loved to hear her say it.

She moved farther away from me. "I'm going to take a shower." Her voice was flat.

My first impulse was to follow her, but I knew this wasn't a great idea. I had to give her space for now.

She took forever in the bathroom. I asked several times whether everything was OK, but she gave me the same answer each time—that she'd be out when she was ready. I let it go. Although I was restless and upset. I wanted to explain my situation to her. Eventually I thought of something that might work better than trying to talk while she was in this kind of mood. I sat down at the desk and searched for a piece of paper and a pen. When I heard her come out of the bathroom, I tucked it all back out of sight.

"I'm going to bed," she said quietly.

I nodded and approached her, wanting to give her a kiss, but I stopped myself and simply said, "Sounds good. Sleep well. My turn for a shower." I backed toward the bathroom. I wanted to watch what she was doing. She didn't look at me. She just got in bed, buried her face into her pillow, and pulled the sheet up to her chin.

I took my time, too. I wanted to avoid seeing her in that kind of temper again. Locked in her own world where nobody was granted access. Later, I tiptoed to the bed and crawled in beside her.

"Samuel?" she murmured in her sleep and turned to me.

"Everything is fine. I'm here," I whispered. "I'm here."

"Samuel . . ." She was dreaming. I took her hand, and she snuggled closer, wrapping her arm around me. I knew I shouldn't be doing this, not after whatever had just happened, but I couldn't let her slip into a nightmare. It soothed her when she was against my warmth.

"Hush, sweetie, I'm here with you," I whispered in her ear and kissed her forehead. I let my lips linger. I needed to feel her one more time. Taste her. Inhale her vanilla scent.

"I love you, Samuel," she murmured in her sleep.

I sighed. She was only dreaming. I seriously doubted she meant it, even if I wanted her to.

Chapter 49
Mia—I Was Allowed to Love

Paris, July 2012

I woke up with a familiar headache. It wasn't a good way to start the day. I blinked until my eyes adjusted to the sun shining on my face. Despite bad weather the day before, today promised to be beautiful. I needed to talk with Samuel. I hadn't given him a chance to explain yesterday, but after getting some sleep, I was ready to listen. Next to me, the bed was empty, but the rumpled sheets told me that he'd slept here.

"Samuel?" I called out. No answer.

In a panic, I jumped out of bed.

"Samuel?" He wasn't in the bathroom—and his backpack was nowhere to be seen. He was gone. He'd left without me.

Suddenly, my chest constricted. The lump in my throat rose. Breathe! I had to do it, not just think about it. Samuel had left. Because of me. Because of her. Whoever she was.

I pressed a hand to the wall to keep myself upright, but my knees gave in anyway, and I sank to the floor. Tears ran down my cheeks. What had I done? He'd wanted to talk, and now he was gone. I couldn't even call him. What with spending twenty-four hours a day together, we hadn't even exchanged phone numbers.

I wiped my cheeks, but tears kept coming. A ragged sob escaped my throat. I hurt. I hurt so much. As if someone had torn out my heart. I should have never have opened my soul to him. If I hadn't, I wouldn't be going through this again. No, this time was actually worse than with Christoph. Samuel had managed to do something that nobody else before him had done.

He had made me forget.
He had made me live.
He had brought me back.

Samuel had reignited my desire to live. I'd experienced joy once again. Laughed once again. Lived once again.

Loved.

I should have told him. I'd known all along.

One day, it all will change. You won't prevent that.

No, I had not been able to prevent that. I'd tried. But my feelings for Samuel had been too intense.

He shouldn't have left me first. I should have left him long ago. I should have left him before he'd known my innermost thoughts.

Samuel had been faster.

I huddled on the hard wooden floor, wishing the world around me would just disappear, and I'd never have to stand up again. I continued to sob, knees drawn tight against my chest. Then, through swollen eyes, I noticed a small gray mound on the desk. Slowly, I hauled myself up and leaned against the wall until I felt steady enough to walk over and look down.

My hat lay there. Underneath it was a piece of folded paper. With trembling fingers, I reached for it.

Mia, my sweetie,

This is where I have to end my voyage with you. I need to continue alone. I have waited far too long already. You may not know it, but you have opened my eyes and helped me do what I need to do.

Please don't be sad . . .

Yes, I am visiting a woman, as you so rightly guessed. Yet it is not "another woman." I am visiting my mother. Or, rather, all I have left of her.

I don't like to talk much about her.

Why?

I always held her responsible for my parents' divorce. She moved back to London and remarried. What was I supposed to think, at fourteen? Especially because she didn't want me to come with her.

I never talked with her again. Now it is too late.

My father gave me a letter in which she explained everything. Had I known the truth earlier, my life would be different now. I really believe I need to do this alone. This is why it drives me crazy every time your cell phone rings.

Mia, don't make the same mistake I made. Just listen to what your family wants to tell you. Don't exclude everyone from your life.

Breathe, Mia! Live, Mia!

With love,

Samuel

The tears that had only just stopped streamed down my cheeks again as I cried even harder than before. I pressed the letter to my heart. Now it made sense why he'd always insisted I speak with my parents.

Chapter 49 ½
Samuel—A Farewell Letter

Vienna, May 2012

I had been sitting in front of the TV for days. It distracted me from thinking about my father. From thinking about his company. That was all over, dead and buried. He could spare himself all the telephone calls. I would never answer. I would never again set foot in his offices. He should have thought about how I'd react before he'd done what he'd done. I was so goddamn angry at him.

The doorbell rang. Slowly, I got up, crossed the room, and opened it, not thinking to first check who was there. It was him . . .

I folded my arms over my chest and blocked the door when he made a move as if to enter. "What do you want, Matthias?" I spat.

"You won't let me in?" He sounded defeated.

"We've nothing left to talk about."

He scratched his forehead. "OK, whatever you want." I waited for something more. Without the slightest emotion, he blurted, "Your mother died two days ago."

Her death meant nothing to me. I answered coldly, "Good for her." At least now she wouldn't be able to get on my nerves anymore.

My father shook his head. "You could at least forgive her now." He pressed a letter into my hand. "I haven't opened it. It was in the mail this morning."

I shoved the yellow envelope into the back pocket of my jeans.

"You can't hold a grudge forever," my father muttered.

"Thank you for delivering my mail. Now, good-bye, Father." I slammed the door.

I pulled out the envelope, sat back down on the couch, and inspected the front of the envelope. No return address. Just an English stamp. I hastily opened the letter.

> Dear Samuel,
> It hurts so badly when your own son has banished you from his life. I am not going to reproach you or make you feel guilty. That's not my intention. But it is true that you never gave me a chance to explain myself.
> I'm afraid now it is too late.
> James left me, your father left me. I am alone. You refuse to see me or even speak with me. Your father did a good job in turning you away from me. I never intended to abandon you. He forced me to.
> Samuel, I am ill. Terminally ill. Cancer . . . The doctors gave me six months. I was hoping you'd relent toward me, but you haven't answered my calls. Nothing from you. Not one sign.
> I don't want to go on like this.
> When you read this, it will be over. I don't want to wait six months for my last day.

I love you, my son.
Mom

Air . . . I needed air! And I needed to run, needed to run far, far from here.

Chapter 50
Samuel—Not Alone

London, July 2012

A strong wind was blowing. I flipped up the hood on my sweatshirt, then zipped the front all the way up until my face was nearly hidden. Other than the sound of the wind, all was quiet. Only a few people walked past me, going where I was not yet ready to go. Mia was right. The farther north we'd traveled, the more I'd struggled with myself and whether or not I should visit here. Because now what good did it do? She couldn't hear me. She couldn't forgive me. She was dead. My mom was dead, goddamn it.

She'd written that she didn't want me to feel guilty, but hell, how could I not? She wasn't responsible for the divorce, like my father had had me believe for all those years. He'd never told me the truth, although I had asked him about the divorce so many times. It must have been his plan, to keep me for himself and for his company. I hated him even more for that.

And what had I done, out of sheer despair? I'd run away from Mia. Then again, I wanted to do this alone. At least that's what I told myself. That's why I'd had to write Mia the note. I hoped she understood. So now I was sitting on this bench near the entrance to the cemetery, alone, and I wasn't strong enough to go inside by myself. Mia had been the toughest one all along. I admired her for how she'd climbed out of the deep hole she'd been in. How she had fought, day after day. How she had begun to live again.

After that night in Paris, once she'd said those three words in her sleep, it had been harder to decide what I should do. I wasn't sure I had faith she'd meant them, but still . . . there must be some truth there. I'd lain awake all night and watched her. She'd slept so peacefully in my arms, and I knew she'd felt sheltered. In the morning, I'd kissed her forehead, grabbed my stuff, and just . . . left.

I'd had a knee-jerk reaction. I should never have gone . . . not like that. I hadn't even given her my phone number. I was a coward. And now afraid she'd choose the same path my mother had. While she was strong and healthy now, she'd only just recovered, and her past had been more than difficult. What if that past caught up with her? Could I return to her, be strong enough to provide support for her again? I was a jerk, like her ex-boyfriend. I disappeared the moment things had gotten tough. I'd likely never see her again. I'd messed the whole thing up. And I'd never meet anyone like Mia again.

I dropped my head back against the stone wall behind me, as if I could knock some sense into myself. Raindrops splattered my face, dripped into my eyes, and ran down my cheeks, like tears. If I waited any longer, I again wouldn't make it to my mother's graveside. Yesterday, I'd not managed to get even this far, and today, I'd spent the entire day just sitting here on this bench, like a douche bag. I closed my eyes to sort out my thoughts.

"You should go inside."

I looked up when I heard the sweet sound of her voice.

She was wearing her hat again. "How long have you been sitting here?"

My heart pounded. I was thrilled to see her. I'd been so stupid to exclude her. I should have known I was not the strong one of the two of us. Mia was and always had been. She knew how this felt, knew how I felt. If anybody could support me in this situation, it was her.

I shrugged, wanting to play it cool. "A while."

Mia sat down beside me, holding her backpack against her. We both stared straight ahead.

"How did you find me?"

"You'd mentioned where she lived. With your letter, it wasn't too difficult to put two and two together." She sounded hurt.

I turned to her, but she continued to keep her gaze forward. "Mia . . ." I let out a deep sigh. "Look, I, uh . . ." I ran my fingers through my hair. "Hell, I am so sorry I left the way I did. But I thought . . . Honestly, I don't know what I was thinking. I wasn't thinking. I just ran."

Finally, she turned her head to look at me. "It's OK. I get it. In certain situations, people want to be alone." She set her backpack on the ground and took my hand. "You aren't the only one who thinks running away is the best solution. But I've come to realize that life's not as bad when we have someone on our side. The support may not solve whatever the problems are, but it makes everything easier to bear."

I intertwined our fingers. "Are you mad at me?"

She glanced at our hands, then looked away again. She sighed softly. "Am I angry?"

I nodded.

"I don't know. Yes. No. Maybe . . ." She looked at the ground and murmured, "I probably would have done the same thing."

The silence between us was uncomfortable. Neither of us dared to look into the other's eyes. I'd screwed up. I knew it. And yet, here she was. Mia wanted to be here for me.

"Samuel," Mia finally broke the silence. "I'm not angry." She returned her gaze to mine. "I am disappointed. Really disappointed. I thought you'd figured out things don't work so well when you're alone. But no, I'm not angry. You've done so much for me."

"How?"

"By just being with me. By letting me be myself. By not mentioning my illness." Tears shimmered in her eyes. "And this," she whispered, leaning toward me. For a fleeting moment, her lips touched mine. "You've shown me how to live. You've made sure I didn't forget to breathe. That I didn't forget to find happiness in each moment." Then she murmured so softly that I almost didn't hear it, "You've shown me how to love."

I didn't know what to say, so instead I gave her a gentle kiss.

"Thank you," I whispered against her lips. "Thank you for being here for me."

A wary smile hovered around her lips.

Mia stood, shrugged her backpack over her shoulder, then looked at me with her big eyes, now glistening with tears. She reached out her hand. "Come on. There's someone you need to visit, I'll bet. Because I'm guessing you've been sitting here all day."

"Only since eight."

"Samuel, that was nine hours ago."

Mia was right. I had to gather my courage and say good-bye to my mother. I nodded and rose. We walked into the cemetery. I'd researched online where she was buried so knew right where to go.

Her grave still looked new, marked only by a pile of recently dug earth. No flowers, no tombstone. Nobody appeared to be tending it, even though it had been a month since the funeral. I just stood there. My mother was gone; she would never come back. I would never be able to speak to her again. Never again . . .

I sank down to the cold ground. I felt a small hand squeezing my shoulder. Mia. Tears filled my eyes.

"It is OK to admit your feelings," she leaned down to whisper in my ear. When I heard her words, I couldn't hold back my emotion any longer.

"I am so sorry, Mom. I am so, so sorry . . ." I whispered over and over again.

"What happened to her?"

Mia's question caught me off guard. I didn't look at her when I answered, "She was ill . . . terminal cancer. She wrote me that the doctors had given her six months. But she didn't want to go on . . . Not the way her life had been. Without her second husband, without my father." I sighed and added, "Without me."

Mia knelt and held me tight. "Don't blame yourself. That was her decision." She sighed. "Hers. Sooner or later . . ." She paused. "It's not your fault," she whispered close to my ear. "You understand?" She wasn't talking about only my mother. I sensed there was more behind what she was saying.

"Mia, you . . . ?"

She shook her head. "No . . ." She inhaled deeply. "Not me." She couldn't continue. She was crying in earnest now. She hid her face against my chest and murmured, "Samuel, please take me home."

Chapter 51
Mia—At Home

Graz, July 2012

The moment at the grave and seeing Samuel's pain forced me to reconsider the decisions I'd made. I had been, in fact, running away, and it'd been the wrong way to handle things. Hurting anybody hadn't been my intention, but I'd ended up hurting everyone. I didn't want to run anymore. It was time I faced my family.

I felt very uncomfortable at even the thought of returning home. I'd been out of touch with my parents and sister for more than three weeks, almost four—and then, of course, I'd also ignored their calls.

Once I could see my parents' house, I asked the cab driver to let me and Samuel out. I didn't want my family to see me right away. I wanted to walk those last yards to their home. I needed time to breathe, to focus.

"Samuel?" There were only a few steps left before we reached the door.

"You can do it, Mia. You're strong. No matter what you're hiding, your family will forgive you." He gave me his sweet smile, the first I'd seen on him in twenty-four hours.

During the last day of our return, on the train, he'd seemed always on alert, watching me constantly. There was fear in his face. I'm sure he was afraid that my panic-induced blackouts would return. By now, though, I had them under control. I'd been feeling much better ever since I'd opened up to him.

Now I tried to flash a smile. "Can you do me a favor?" I asked.

"Anything. You were there for me, too. Remember?" He reached for my hand, pulled me toward him, and kissed my forehead.

"Will you stay with me?"

He nodded.

"I mean, no matter what happens here, please, please, don't abandon me. No matter what I say, what they say, please stand by me." I took a ragged breath. "Promise?"

Samuel lifted my chin with his thumb and index finger. "Sweetie, I will always be here for you. I left you in Paris. But that'll be the last time. From now on, I will always be here for you. *Always* . . ." Almost inaudibly, he added, "I've already let down someone else." He frowned, and I knew he was thinking of his mother. "We are so closely linked, you and me. I don't want to miss out on anything else with you." His soft lips again touched mine. He whispered, "I live through you. Don't forget that."

I just nodded. My heart was racing as I stood in front of my family's old brown wooden door. How many times had I walked through this same door, in an earlier life without problems, without fear? And now here I was—a nervous wreck. Hands wet with sweat. About to suffer a panic attack after all, because I had no idea what awaited me inside.

"Breathe, Mia. Live, Mia," Samuel encouraged me and gave me a kiss. I tightened my grip on his hand. "I am right here with you," he said.

My other hand trembled.

With a lot of effort, I managed to insert my key into the lock and open the door. We entered. At first the house seemed deathly silent. The only things I could hear were the sounds of my heart beating in my ears and the huff of my breath. Slowly, I distinguished others. Someone was emptying the dishwasher. Music drifted down the stairs.

I led Samuel into the kitchen. Her back to us, Mother was putting a plate into the cupboard. She hadn't noticed us yet. I stopped in the doorway.

"Mom," I interrupted the quiet. The plate she'd been holding dropped from her hand and shattered on the floor. She whipped around, grabbing the edge of the countertop.

"Oh my god, Mia." Recovering, she hurried over and hugged me with all her might, but my hand still clung to Samuel's. "You're OK!" she sobbed and cupped my face with both hands. "Are you OK?"

I'd missed her so much. My sunshine. Tears shot into my eyes. I had a huge lump in my throat and couldn't say a word. I could only nod.

"That's good," she said and hugged me close again. "I worried so much about you," she whispered. My blouse was dampened by her tears. And mine.

"I'm here, Mom. I'm OK, Mom." I soothed her, embracing her with one arm and leaning my head against hers. I didn't want to let go. I wanted her to know that I was back for real. That I loved her. That I was sorry. Hoping she could sense my emotions, I held her as tight and as long as I could.

Several minutes passed, then her head jerked up. She looked at me in bewilderment. "You . . . How come you let me hug you for so long? And you're even hugging me back? *How come?*"

I smiled and released her. "Mom, this is Samuel. He's the reason why." Only then did she seem to notice him.

She stretched out her hand. "Irene. It's very nice to meet you, Mr. . . . ?"

"Winter. Very nice to meet you, too. Please call me Samuel."

She smiled, then went to call my father and my sister, who were overjoyed and emotional, too. Eventually, after the noise of our reunion subsided and after Mom made coffee, we all sat down in the living room.

"Don't you want to introduce your companion?" The way Anna grinned at Samuel was a little too flirty for my taste. I already knew his impact on women, but my little sister didn't need to undress him with her eyes.

I kicked her shin. "Anna," I hissed.

She leaned close to me and whispered, "You've seen him, right? You're sitting next to the hottest guy ever. Oh my god, those eyes. If you don't want him, I'll take him."

I was pretty sure Samuel could hear my sister because I felt his body shake as he apparently tried to suppress his laughter. But she was right—and not just about how he looked—I'd formally introduced him only to my mother. Besides, I owed all of them a fuller explanation. I took Samuel's hand. "This is Samuel Winter. He is . . ." I looked at him.

"I'm her boyfriend." He squeezed my hand. Relieved, I smiled. Yes, he was my boyfriend.

Anna seemed disappointed but then gave me a grin.

"We met on the first train I took, the train to Budapest, and ran into each other again when we were both headed to Rome. He's rescued me more than once from panic attacks. He gave me space when I needed it. He cheered me up when I needed it. Made me feel again. Made me believe again that it's normal to hold and touch another human being." While I said this, I looked into his eyes. A brief silence followed after I finished.

My father cleared his throat. "I'm very glad to see you so happy, Mia. But we've been very worried."

I looked at the floor and began biting my lip.

"We didn't know what was going on. Why didn't you call?"

"I . . . I don't know," I lied.

"Please, don't ever do this again," my mother implored. "Promise, Mia."

"I promise," I whispered.

Chapter 52
Samuel—So That Was It?

Graz, July 2012

I was very glad Mia had decided to return to her family. I wouldn't have been able to deal with her not wanting to go back. Her parents must have been worried to death, not hearing a word for three weeks. And it seemed she had a great relationship with them. But now, finally, she was back.

"Samuel?" We were cuddling in her bed. I shifted so we were facing each other. "How long do you want to stay?" She pushed some strands of hair from my forehead.

"As long as you want me to, sweetie."

A smile curved at her lips. "As long as I want you to?"

"As long as you want me to," I repeated. "I've already told you that I will always be here for you."

Mia snuggled closer and murmured against my chest, "You're my boyfriend. I still can't believe it."

I raised her head with my index finger under her chin. "What is there not to believe?"

She rolled onto her stomach and propped herself up on her elbows. "You've seen how I can be, Samuel. I mean, three weeks ago I wouldn't even let you touch me, and now this." She beamed. "You've conquered my heart. You've made me feel again."

I shook my head. "No, Mia. It wasn't me. It was you. I was just there to accompany you. You did it all yourself." With my fingertip, I drew small circles on the bare skin of her back. She was wearing only a bra and panties. I could see her flesh goose bump. How I loved it when my touch made her shiver.

"I did it. I made it," she repeated my words, rolled toward me again, and began caressing my chest, then kissed her way across it and up to my mouth. She nibbled my lower lip. I tightened my grip around her. Then she licked the crease between my lips. My hands wandered down her spine until I cupped the flesh of her nicely shaped butt.

A soft moan escaped her. She climbed on top of me, her hips soon undulating. Hard now, I clasped her tighter. She seemed to like the strength of my grip. I could tell by the way she pressed against me. "If you go on like this"—I panted—"it will be over soon."

She wore a broad grin and shifted until she was kneeling next to me. I started to speak, but she shushed me with an index finger over my lips. Her eyes shone brightly. She opened her bra and then removed her panties. Hardly able to stand it, I sat up and pulled her close. I enjoyed the warmth of her bare flesh. She softly caressed my skin and kissed every inch of my body. Then she slid one hand around my penis and gently moved her fist up and down. After awhile, unable to take much more, I rolled us over so she was now the one lying on her back. Softly, I stroked her inner thighs. I drew a nipple into my mouth. She moaned, and I released it only so I could kiss a path down her torso to her core. I let my tongue tend to her sensitive flesh. She arched against my touch. Her hands tangled in my hair. Then she pulled me up and devoured my mouth. I positioned myself between her legs and tenderly penetrated her. Then there was only our panting, and the mad beating of our hearts. We grew oblivious, lost in each other, and then we came. Shudders still gripping me, I finally relaxed against her. As her hot breath singed my skin, I smoothed her hair.

"I love to feel your heart beat so wildly," she murmured, and as I slid off her, she let her lips glide across my chest.

"My heart beats wildly because of you, Mia. It lives through you. I live through you." Mia seemed to focus all her attention on me. "I felt so empty. Now you are here, and I'm filled with life." I caressed her cheek. "I'm so happy I found you," I whispered. This was more than love. This was life itself.

"I know what you mean." Mia wrapped her arms tightly around me, then she drew back and captured my gaze. "I feel the same." Her eyes grew wet, but no tears escaped. She seemed to be holding them in. "I live through you, Samuel. And so much more."

"I know, Mia." My eyelids drooped. It had been a long day, and I felt so awed, so replete lying here with her.

"I wish I had met you sooner," I heard her say. This time, I knew I heard her correctly.

The sun woke me, shining directly in my face. Mia was sleeping, her back to me. I let my fingers run down her spine. She didn't react. The trip home must have exhausted her. I moved closer, wanting to hug her, but drew back alarmed when I noticed her body was cool under my touch. Something was wrong.

"Mia? Mia, can you hear me?"

I shook her shoulder, and she tumbled onto her back. Panic coursed through me. With trembling fingers, I felt for her pulse. It was far too weak. What was happening? No, no . . . This must be a dream.

I shook her again, but she still didn't respond. I jumped out of bed. I needed my phone, now. Where was it? In my backpack. Frantically, I grabbed it up, searched through it, and finally found the instrument and punched some numbers.

Everything was taking too long! It must have rung ten times before someone answered.

"I need help!" I blurted. "My girlfriend, she's hardly breathing. Her pulse is too slow."

"Calm down. Did she take anything?" the dispatcher asked.

"No, no, she didn't. I have no idea what's going on. Please send an ambulance. Now!"

"We need your address."

"I—I only know the name of the street but not the number." I gave it to them. As for the number, I didn't want to leave Mia alone to run down and look. Nobody else was home. Her parents had said they both had to leave for work early today, and her sister was at her internship.

"Stay calm. Do you know approximately where the house is located?"

"Yes . . . near the end of the street. A brown front door. No fence. Next to an empty lot," I stammered.

"We'll be right there. Stay with your girlfriend."

Quickly, I jumped into my clothes and covered Mia with a sheet.

"Everything will be fine. The ambulance is coming any minute," I said over and over again. I touched her cheeks. They were cold. She was cold. And she wouldn't wake up.

The paramedics arrived promptly and pulled me away from Mia. "Please step to the side. You can meet us at the hospital."

I didn't want to leave her alone. "Let me come with you, please. I'm not from here, and I don't have a car," I begged. "Please."

"OK," one of the paramedics agreed. "Hurry up."

It was chaos. They gave her artificial respiration, but her heartbeat apparently slowed even more. Then they began cardiac massage, relaying what they were doing into a radio, using terms I'd never heard and hadn't ever wanted to hear. I only wanted my Mia back. She couldn't die.

Chapter 52 ½
Mia—I'll Just Run Away

Graz, June 2012

I was very nervous that day, knowing I would receive the results from my most recent checkup. After the previous exam, everything had looked good, but I always felt awkward meeting with Dr. Oberbichler. He had been my doctor since the beginning, but I didn't like him. It wasn't his fault—it was just that he reminded me of the day my life had shattered.

I knocked and entered his office. My knees were weak.

"Take a seat, Ms Lang," he said, indicating a chair across from his desk. "I'll be with you in a minute. Just need to sign these papers . . ." When he finally looked up, I knew he had bad news. He was frowning, and his jaw was tense. He repeatedly clicked the end of his pen, which made me even more nervous. I picked my cuticle. It hurt, but I knew that what I was about to hear would hurt even more.

"This is the most difficult part of my job," he began.

Wanting to deny what was coming, I shook my head. I knew it. I covered my mouth to suppress a sob.

"Listen to me."

I just kept shaking my head. But I could hear damned well what he was saying.

"I am really sorry to tell you this, but unfortunately, your therapy hasn't been entirely successful. A new tumor has begun to grow, and—"

"No, don't tell me where," I interrupted. "I don't want to know." My words sounded faint, even to me.

"Ms. Lang," he sighed and straightened in his chair. "We can get rid of this with another operation and a new round of chemo."

I shook my head. My heart was beating loud, the sound of it pounding in my ears. "How long?" I asked bleakly.

"Nobody talks about dying here. You can live—"

"How long?" I interrupted again, this time in a much sharper voice.

"If we don't act, I can't guarantee anything—days, weeks, months. The tumor must have grown fast, otherwise we would have discovered it during the previous exam. But it needs to be removed. It's pressing against—"

I raised my right hand. "I told you I don't want to know." I moaned. I would not be able to endure going through everything all over again.

"Ms. Lang—"

"No," I snapped. "No, Dr. Oberbichler. Do you have any idea how much I suffered? Do you know what I've been through? No, you don't," I hissed. "I don't want to be like that again. Nauseated all the time. Nobody knows how to deal with me. I hate myself. I'm trying to accept what life remains for me, to make sense of everything that has happened. I had even begun to think that maybe, maybe, I might return to normalcy." I lowered my voice. "But, no. No, it's not meant to be. It was never meant to be. The only thing that's meant is for me to vanish from this earth. You don't get a second chance. I had mine, for one year. One more year to live." I bit my lower lip and tasted the blood on my tongue. "If you can call this living. And now . . ."

Dr. Oberbichler looked at me intently before he continued. "It would give you even more time. The prognosis is very good, provided we act soon."

I got up. "From now on, I will be in charge of my life. Not a tumor. And not you." I headed for the door.

"This is not our last conversation, Mia. I won't give up on you," Dr. Oberbichler called after me. "Take some time to think about it. But I won't give up on you."

"But I do," I whispered and walked out the room.

My gut feeling had been right. I'd just known things would not end well. I had to leave. I didn't want to be a burden to my family again. I wanted them to remember me as Mia. As the Mia I had once been. Maybe even that wasn't possible anymore, but at least they could remember me as someone with a future. Someone who was healed. I would not tell a soul.

That same day, I finally took Dr. Weiß's advice to heart. He was right. I had to go away. I didn't want to. I now hated change, and this trip would be nothing but change, day after day. In my old life, I'd loved tackling challenges. Not anymore. But I also knew I wouldn't be able to hide my secret if I stayed. My mother would realize something was wrong. The only solution was to run off and embark on the "trip of my life" as soon as possible.

Chapter 53
Samuel—Nothing

Graz, July 2012

I'd been sitting in the bleak waiting room for more than an hour, my head buried in my hands, wondering what on earth had happened. Just the night before, everything had seemed OK.

Two doctors had been waiting when the ambulance pulled up in front of the hospital. They tore open the doors and yanked on the stretcher as the paramedics jumped out. The doctors busied themselves over Mia, feeling for her pulse. I was useless. Watching helplessly as Mia was rolled away from me, I remained inside. I'd never forget the sight of her lifeless body. The image was burned onto my retinas. She'd looked as if she were already dead.

No, no. This couldn't be. They had to revive her. They had to. I couldn't.

"I need to go with her," I said, suddenly regaining some sense. I jumped down from the ambulance and started after her, but a paramedic grabbed my arm.

"You can't go that way. Go through that door, to the waiting room."

I stared at him. I couldn't stay with her? At least wait outside the operating room or wherever they took her?

"Go to the waiting room," he repeated. "The doctors know what they're doing. Everything will be OK."

I nodded and went where he'd pointed.

Not long after I took a seat in the waiting room, Mia's parents rushed in. "What happened?" her mother asked. Her cheeks were smudged with black mascara from her tears.

I shook my head. "I have no idea. This morning when I woke up, she was just lying there, unconscious. She was hardly breathing." I ran one hand through my hair and rubbed my face. Just the thought of it . . . I was about to cry.

"Oh my god, I am so glad you were there." Irene hugged me, and I patted her back. "Who knows what would have happened . . ." She couldn't finish the sentence and burst into tears. Mia's father neared and grasped his wife's shoulder. She turned around and buried her face in his chest. Peter held her tight while guiding her to one of the chairs, then embraced her until her tears subsided. I felt so alone—Mia had been taken away from me.

After a long time, a young doctor entered. Peter looked up as she started toward them and jogged Irene's shoulder to get Mia's mother's attention. The doctor sat down next to Peter.

"Are you Miss Lang's parents?"

Both nodded, apparently beyond speech.

"I am Dr. Ramhofer," she said. I moved to a chair that was closer to them. Peter was holding Irene's hand, stroking the back with his thumb. The doctor's expression revealed nothing. "Your daughter is unconscious. We are giving her artificial respiration."

A sob escaped Mia's mother.

The doctor squeezed her hand. "We are doing everything we can, Mrs. Lang. Is there any medical history we should know about?"

Mia's father summarized what had occurred over the past twelve months.

The doctor nodded. "Thank you. I will contact the oncology department." Then she stood. "We will keep you updated." She left.

Irene wrapped her arms around her husband's neck. He whispered something in her ear.

I ran after the doctor. "Dr. Ramhofer, please, wait a second."

"What can I do for you?" she asked.

"I'm Ms. Lang's boyfriend," I said. "Was that the whole story? There must be more to it."

The doctor just looked at me.

I lowered my voice and asked, "What's really going on?" My despair must have been palpable.

But the doctor only smiled at me sadly and turned.

"Please," I begged.

She paused. Waited. Hesitated. Then she shook her head, looked at the floor, and walked away.

This couldn't be happening. My mouth was dry. It felt as if all the blood had rushed to my head. My heart was racing. No . . . no! I must be dreaming. The world that had opened up for me over the past several weeks was annihilated.

Mia had become the center of my life. She'd encouraged me to visit my mother's grave. She'd made me come alive. She was the stronger one of us. She was my love.

Mia had to breathe.
Mia had to live.

Chapter 54

Samuel—A Goddamn Miserable Year

Cemetery, August 2013

The past year had been the most miserable of my life. I'd never suffered so much. I'd never seen so much suffering.

I never left Graz. How could I? I couldn't abandon Mia's family, so we all endured the months together. Mia was a part of us. She was a part of me. Without her, I wasn't whole anymore.

Nobody had been prepared for this situation. Nobody had imagined it would happen. Nobody, except Mia . . .

Mia had known all along. She'd seen it coming, but she'd run away, deluding herself into believing she was taking her therapist's advice. But she'd never really wanted to leave her loved ones behind. Too, she'd always been afraid to venture out from her sheltered world. Until she found something else to be even more afraid of—that she would have to bear the same pain she'd already experienced, all over again, alone. So she'd run.

Mia hadn't told a soul about the new diagnosis. She'd allowed everyone to believe she was doing fine. Her family had believed it. I'd believed it. She'd seemed happy. Maybe this was why: she'd wanted to feel alive one last time, overcome her fears, and enjoy each moment. And she had, for three weeks, and I'd been privileged to be a part of that.

But as much as I loved her, I was also angry at her. She'd made me believe there'd be a happy ending. I resented that she'd drawn me into this situation without giving me a hint of what I was up against. Then again, when we'd first met, I'd not told her about my mother, either.

Oh, damn it . . . I should have figured it out. There were fragments of time—sentences, a touch, expressions—that had hinted at the truth. I just hadn't understood their full meaning.

The pain of remembering tore me apart. Then I began blaming myself. Why had I not picked up on such hints? But how could I? Especially at the beginning, I didn't really know her that well. Even her parents hadn't sensed anything. Mia had hid her new turmoil well.

That we hadn't grasped the truth wasn't anyone's fault. Mia had planned for us not to. The only thing she hadn't planned was to involve another person. Me . . .

It was difficult to see her in the hospital, lying there, chained to the respiratory machine. I could hardly bear it. My sweetie was so helpless. I just hoped she wasn't in pain.

Her condition was critical. The removal of the new tumor was successful, but after that, she hadn't recovered, and her condition had worsened. She was put in an induced coma. Viruses plagued her. We watched helplessly as she grew weaker and weaker each day. The doctors prepared her family and me for the worst.

Her mother and I spent whole days at her bedside. Sometimes we cried together, and other times we just sat in a silence, broken only by the wheezing of the machines that were keeping her alive.

"Samuel, was she happy?" Irene asked me one afternoon. I took my eyes off Mia. "Was she happy?" Irene repeated.

I sucked in a breath. "Yes, she was happy," I said and smiled, remembering. "She laughed a lot. She enjoyed everything we did. She basked in the sunshine. She heard every sound around us. She seemed at peace."

A sad smile hovered over Irene's face. Tears filled her eyes. "At least it's good to know she was granted that joy. Thank you for making it possible." Irene hugged me a long time.

A year had passed. I was so glad to know Mia's family, to have their support and give them mine. This was what made a family, and I was a part of theirs now.

I stood outside the cemetery in London. It had been almost exactly a year since I'd visited my mother's grave that first time. I remembered what a tremendously difficult journey it had been to get here. Guilt and remorse still haunted me. Would I feel differently had I known my mother better? Or would I feel the same? I could no longer hold back my tears and searched for a tissue in the pocket of my leather coat. I found one, but I also found something else. A piece of paper. The upper edge was ruffled. It looked as if it had been torn hastily from a notebook. It was a letter from Mia.

Samuel,
When you read this, I will be gone.
Maybe you can imagine where I am. Maybe you knew all along what I was up to. ~~I wanted to leave.~~

I ran away from reality. But I always knew reality would catch up with me sooner or later. Sooner, I was afraid. And then our fight . . . On one hand, I'm glad you want to continue by yourself. You have touched my life. Too much. I came to like you. Too much. It became more. ~~I fell in love~~. That would make everything even more difficult. I'd almost changed my plans. ~~For someone I don't even know very well.~~ For you! ~~You have changed my life.~~ You've almost become my life . . . But I did not want to drag you into this. I didn't want to hurt anybody. All I wanted was to live again for a short while, before everything was over.

It was the most beautiful ending I could have asked for.

Thank you!
With love,
Mia

I hadn't worn this coat since that long-ago night in Paris. She must have written the letter the same evening I'd written mine to her.

I felt the touch of her hand on my shoulder.

"What are you reading?" she asked.

I stood and hugged her. "I'm so glad you followed me to London." I held her face between my hands and kissed her forehead. I looked into her wonderful, shining emerald eyes. "I'm so grateful you're right here with me."

Mia smiled and gave me a kiss. "I'll always support you as best as I can. I will always be at your side. I will always come with you to your mother's grave." She kissed me again. "You're the reason I fought my way back. Without you, I wouldn't be here anymore. Thank you."

Gently, I stroked her short hair. She didn't wear a hat anymore. She accepted that there were days when she didn't feel well, and she was no longer ashamed of herself. She had outgrown her fears this past year and grown even stronger as a person. I'd always believed she could reach any goal she set for herself. And she had. She'd battled and defeated cancer not only once but twice.

Her hospital stay had seemed to last forever. They'd kept her in an induced coma for three weeks. After they woke her, she'd been tormented by pain. It had been unbearable, watching her suffer so much. But she was tough. She'd wanted to make it. She'd gritted her teeth, taken each blow and each pain in stride. Her family and I had her back. The objective was clear: Mia wanted to continue her—our—trip where it had ended a year ago.

I was so proud of her. I'd never let her go.

Chapter 55
Mia—A New Life

London, August 2013

Samuel held me in his arms. He'd never leave. He'd stuck by me throughout the past year. I loved him for that.

After I read his farewell letter in Paris, I'd been so very angry. Angry . . . sad . . . disappointed. Running away wasn't him. He was courageous—I was the one who ran. My letter . . .

Actually, I'd wanted to break up. For hours, I'd pondered whether continuing with him was the right thing to do. Finally, I gave into my heart and decided I wanted to stay with him. I couldn't wait to tell him everything. Then I fell asleep . . . and when I woke, he was gone. And with him, the letter I'd written.

I'd sat all day in the same spot in the hotel room, trying to figure out why he felt he had to go alone. Perhaps because he was stubborn, like me. After all, I'd wanted exactly the same thing—to be alone while I took charge of my own life. At least that's what I'd made myself believe.

Had I been mad at him? Of course! He'd left without talking things through with me. I'd opened up to him and confided almost every detail of my ordeal. He knew how much I'd suffered when Christoph and Julia betrayed me, so at first I thought he was no better than them. Then I realized he was just stubborn. From the beginning, his goal had been to visit his mother's grave. Alone. Then I'd appeared, completely not according to his plan, and he wanted to finish alone what he'd started out to do.

I'd been unable to stay mad at him for long. I understood him far too well. So I began searching for him and figured out he was going to his mother's grave and where it was. I knew he needed my support. By then I'd realized we didn't need to manage everything by ourselves. The situation would be easier with a friend by his side.

After I'd found him, after we'd walked into the cemetery and I'd watched him kneel beside his mother's grave, devastated, I realized I couldn't inflict this same pain on my family. Not after Samuel had shown me how to live. How to love.

My decision had been clear. I wanted to go home. Tell them everything. And live. But things had gone downhill too fast, before I could tell them anything.

For a while after I'd woke from my coma, I didn't remember that day in London. In fact, I didn't remember much of the three weeks traveling across Europe. I remembered only the painful weeks after the latest operation. My worst fears came true: chemotherapy. Nausea and vomiting. No appetite. Hair loss.

The difference was that once I did remember, I really wanted to survive. I had a goal. I had support. I had Samuel . . .

I was happy. I'd received another chance. The path ahead wasn't an easy one, but my future was well worth fighting for, no matter how difficult the battle. As long as I remembered to *breathe* and to *live*.

Samuel kissed my forehead and smiled at me. "What were you thinking?"

I grinned and snuggled up against him. Inhaled his fresh smell, which I'd grown to love. "I was thinking of everything that happened during the past year. I am so happy, Samuel. I'm so grateful you were—are—at my side. I fought for us and always will."

Softly, he caressed my cheek. "Anytime, sweetie. And I will *always* be here for you."

He lowered his head and kissed me. Wearing that sweet smile of his, he whispered, "I love you, Mia. I live through you."

Those words made me fight every new day. "I love you, Samuel. I live through you."

About the Author

Elisabeth Wagner lives with her husband and two children in eastern Austria. She published her first book, *Grenzenlos*, in Germany. *Drawn to Life* is her second novel. For more information, visit her at www.elisabethwagner.at.

About the Translator

Julia Knobloch is a translator, writer, and producer. She moved to Brooklyn four years ago and translates fiction and nonfiction for AmazonCrossing and individual clients, from German to English and from English, Spanish, French and Portuguese to German. Julia's TV documentaries on scientific exploration, adventure expeditions, and WWII history have aired on the National Geographic Channel, Discovery Channel, ABC, and German public broadcasting. Her writing has appeared in major German and Argentine newspapers and magazines and online with Open Democracy and The Brooklyn Rail.